DOVER · THRIFT · EDITIONS

Julius Caesar

WILLIAM SHAKESPEARE

Dover Publications, Inc.
New York

DOVER THRIFT EDITIONS

GENERAL EDITOR: STANLEY APPELBAUM
EDITOR OF THIS VOLUME: SHANE WELLER

Performance

This Dover Thrift Edition may be used in its entirety, in adaptation or in any other way for theatrical productions, professional and amateur, in the United States, without fee, permission or acknowledgment. (This may not apply outside of the United States, as copyright conditions may vary.)

This Dover edition, first published in 1991, contains the unabridged text of *Julius Caesar* as published in Volume XV of *The Caxton Edition of the Complete Works of William Shakespeare*, Caxton Publishing Company, London, n.d.

Manufactured in the United States of America
Dover Publications, Inc., 31 East 2nd Street, Mineola, N.Y. 11501

Library of Congress Cataloging-in-Publication Data

Shakespeare, William, 1564–1616.
Julius Caesar / William Shakespeare.
p. cm. — (Dover thrift editions)
ISBN 0-486-26876-4 (pbk.)
1. Caesar, Julius—Drama.
2. Rome—History—53–44 B.C.—Drama.
I. Title. II. Series.
PR2808.A1 1991
822.3'3—dc20 91-14338
CIP

Note

FIRST PERFORMED in the fall of 1599 at the newly built Globe Theatre in London's Southwark district on the south bank of the Thames, *Julius Caesar* marks the midpoint of William Shakespeare's (1564–1616) career as a dramatist. As his historical source on the assassination of the great Roman statesman, general and author Julius Caesar in 44 B.C., and the subsequent defeat of the conspirators on the battlefield at Philippi, Macedonia, in 42 B.C., Shakespeare relies upon Sir Thomas North's *Lives of the noble Grecians and Romanes* (1579). North's work is an English translation (based on Jacques Amyot's French version) of the Greek biographer Plutarch's *Parallel Lives*. It is interesting to note that Shakespeare follows North's phraseology far more closely than he had that of Raphael Holinshed, whose *Chronicles* (1587) had been his principal source when writing the English history plays.

Julius Caesar is in many respects an epilogue to the English histories of the 1590's and a prologue to the great tragedies of the first decade of the seventeenth century. It shares many of the themes of the earlier histories, exploring the genesis and effects of popular unrest, struggles for political power and civil war. The play is also, however, a moving and ambiguous study of personal tragedy in the figure of Marcus Brutus, and of the seemingly irreconcilable conflicts between friendship and duty, moral integrity and political strength.

Contents

Dramatis Personae

JULIUS CAESAR.
OCTAVIUS CAESAR, MARCUS ANTONIUS, M. AEMIL. LEPIDUS, triumvirs after the death of Julius Caesar.
CICERO, PUBLIUS, POPILIUS LENA, senators.
MARCUS BRUTUS, CASSIUS, CASCA, TREBONIUS, LIGARIUS, DECIUS BRUTUS, METELLUS CIMBER, CINNA, conspirators against Julius Caesar.
FLAVIUS and MARULLUS, tribunes.
ARTEMIDORUS of Cnidos, a teacher of Rhetoric.
A Soothsayer.
CINNA, a poet. Another Poet.
LUCILIUS, TITINIUS, MESSALA, YOUNG CATO, VOLUMNIUS, friends to Brutus and Cassius.
VARRO, CLITUS, CLAUDIUS, STRATO, LUCIUS, DARDANIUS, servants to Brutus.
PINDARUS, servant to Cassius.
CALPURNIA, wife to Caesar.
PORTIA, wife to Brutus.

Senators, Citizens, Guards, Attendants, &c.

SCENE: *Rome; the neighbourhood of Sardis; the neighbourhood of Philippi*

Julius Caesar

Act I—Scene I—Rome

A STREET

Enter FLAVIUS, MARULLUS, *and certain* Commoners.

FLAV. Hence! home, you idle creatures, get you home:
Is this a holiday? what! know you not,
Being mechanical,[1] you ought not walk
Upon a labouring day without the sign
Of your profession? Speak, what trade art thou?

FIRST COM. Why, sir, a carpenter.

MAR. Where is thy leather apron and thy rule?
What dost thou with thy best apparel on?
You, sir, what trade are you?

SEC. COM. Truly, sir, in respect of[2] a fine workman, I am but, as you would say, a cobbler.[3]

MAR. But what trade art thou? answer me directly.

SEC. COM. A trade, sir, that, I hope, I may use with a safe conscience; which is indeed, sir, a mender of bad soles.[4]

MAR. What trade, thou knave? thou naughty knave, what trade?

SEC. COM. Nay, I beseech you, sir, be not out[5] with me: yet, if you be out,[6] sir, I can mend you.

MAR. What mean'st thou by that? mend me, thou saucy fellow!

1. *mechanical*] of the class of mechanic or artisan.
2. *in respect of*] as compared with.
3. *cobbler*] The word is used quibblingly in the sense of "botcher," clumsy worker.
4. *soles*] a favorite pun on "souls."
5. *be not out*] do not lose your temper.
6. *be out*] have worn-out shoes.

SEC. COM. Why, sir, cobble you.

FLAV. Thou art a cobbler, art thou?

SEC. COM. Truly, sir, all that I live by is with the awl: I meddle with no tradesman's matters, nor women's matters, but with awl. I am indeed, sir, a surgeon to old shoes; when they are in great danger, I re-cover them. As proper men as ever trod upon neats-leather[7] have gone upon my handiwork.

FLAV. But wherefore art not in thy shop to-day?
Why dost thou lead these men about the streets?

SEC. COM. Truly, sir, to wear out their shoes, to get myself into more work. But indeed, sir, we make holiday, to see Caesar and to rejoice in his triumph.

MAR. Wherefore rejoice? What conquest brings he home?
What tributaries follow him to Rome,
To grace in captive bonds his chariot-wheels?
You blocks, you stones, you worse than senseless things!
O you hard hearts, you cruel men of Rome,
Knew you not Pompey? Many a time and oft
Have you climb'd up to walls and battlements,
To towers and windows, yea, to chimney-tops,
Your infants in your arms, and there have sat
The live-long day with patient expectation
To see great Pompey pass the streets of Rome:
And when you saw his chariot but appear,
Have you not made an universal shout,
That Tiber trembled underneath her banks
To hear the replication[8] of your sounds
Made in her concave shores?
And do you now put on your best attire?
And do you now cull out a holiday?
And do you now strew flowers in his way
That comes in triumph over Pompey's blood?[9]
Be gone!
Run to your houses, fall upon your knees,
Pray to the gods to intermit the plague
That needs must light on this ingratitude.

FLAV. Go, go, good countrymen, and, for this fault,
Assemble all the poor men of your sort;
Draw them to Tiber banks and weep your tears

7. *neats-leather*] cowhide or calfskin.
8. *replication*] reverberation, echo.
9. *Pompey's blood*] Pompey's sons.

Into the channel, till the lowest stream
Do kiss the most exalted shores of all.[10]

[*Exeunt all the* Commoners.]

See, whether their basest metal be not moved;
They vanish tongue-tied in their guiltiness.
Go you down that way towards the Capitol;
This way will I: disrobe the images,
If you do find them deck'd with ceremonies.[11]

MAR. May we do so?
You know it is the feast of Lupercal.[12]

FLAV. It is no matter; let no images
Be hung with Caesar's trophies. I'll about,
And drive away the vulgar from the streets:
So do you too, where you perceive them thick.
These growing feathers pluck'd from Caesar's wing
Will make him fly an ordinary pitch,[13]
Who else would soar above the view of men
And keep us all in servile fearfulness. [*Exeunt.*]

Scene II—A public place

Flourish. Enter CAESAR; ANTONY, *for the course;*[1] CALPURNIA, PORTIA, DECIUS, CICERO, BRUTUS, CASSIUS, *and* CASCA; *a great crowd following, among them a* Soothsayer.

CAES. Calpurnia!
CASCA. Peace, ho! Caesar speaks. [*Music ceases.*]
CAES. Calpurnia!
CAL. Here, my lord.
CAES. Stand you directly in Antonius' way,
When he doth run his course. Antonius!
ANT. Caesar, my lord?
CAES. Forget not, in your speed, Antonius,

10. *most exalted shores of all*] high-water mark.
11. *ceremonies*] festival ornaments.
12. *the feast of Lupercal*] the Lupercalia, a very ancient festival of purification annually celebrated at Rome in February.
13. *pitch*] a common term in falconry for the highest stage of the falcon's flight.

1. *for the course*] as a priest of Lupercus, equipped for running at the feast of the Lupercalia.

To touch Calpurnia; for our elders say,
The barren, touched in this holy chase,
Shake off their sterile curse.

ANT. I shall remember:
When Caesar says "do this," it is perform'd.

CAES. Set on,[2] and leave no ceremony out. [*Flourish.*]

SOOTH. Caesar!

CAES. Ha! who calls?

CASCA. Bid every noise be still: peace yet again!

CAES. Who is it in the press[3] that calls on me?
I hear a tongue, shriller than all the music,
Cry "Caesar." Speak; Caesar is turn'd to hear.

SOOTH. Beware the ides of March.[4]

CAES. What man is that?

BRU. A soothsayer bids you beware the ides of March.

CAES. Set him before me; let me see his face.

CAS. Fellow, come from the throng; look upon Caesar.

CAES. What say'st thou to me now? speak once again.

SOOTH. Beware the ides of March.

CAES. He is a dreamer;[5] let us leave him: pass.
[*Sennet. Exeunt all but* BRUTUS *and* CASSIUS.]

CAS. Will you go see the order of the course?

BRU. Not I.

CAS. I pray you, do.

BRU. I am not gamesome:[6] I do lack some part
Of that quick spirit[7] that is in Antony.
Let me not hinder, Cassius, your desires;
I'll leave you.

CAS. Brutus, I do observe you now of late:
I have not from your eyes that gentleness
And show of love as I was wont to have:
You bear too stubborn and too strange a hand
Over[8] your friend that loves you.

BRU. Cassius,

2. *Set on*] proceed.
3. *press*] crowd.
4. *the ides of March*] March 15, the midpoint of the month in the Roman calendar.
5. *dreamer*] visionary.
6. *gamesome*] sportive.
7. *quick spirit*] high spirit, liveliness.
8. *You bear . . . a hand Over*] The metaphor is from a horseman's domineering treatment of his steed.

Be not deceived: if I have veil'd my look,
I turn the trouble of my countenance
Merely[9] upon myself. Vexed I am
Of late with passions of some difference,[10]
Conceptions only proper to myself,
Which give some soil[11] perhaps to my behaviours;
But let not therefore my good friends be grieved—
Among which number, Cassius, be you one—
Nor construe any further my neglect
Than that poor Brutus with himself at war
Forgets the shows of love to other men.

CAS. Then, Brutus, I have much mistook your passion;
By means whereof[12] this breast of mine hath buried
Thoughts of great value, worthy cogitations.
Tell me, good Brutus, can you see your face?

BRU. No, Cassius; for the eye sees not itself
But by reflection, by some other things.

CAS. 'T is just:
And it is very much lamented, Brutus,
That you have no such mirrors as will turn
Your hidden worthiness into your eye,
That you might see your shadow.[13] I have heard
Where many of the best respect in Rome,
Except immortal Caesar, speaking of Brutus,
And groaning underneath this age's yoke,
Have wish'd that noble Brutus had his eyes.

BRU. Into what dangers would you lead me, Cassius,
That you would have me seek into myself
For that which is not in me?

CAS. Therefore, good Brutus, be prepared to hear:
And since you know you cannot see yourself
So well as by reflection, I your glass
Will modestly discover to yourself
That of yourself which you yet know not of.
And be not jealous on[14] me, gentle Brutus:
Were I a common laugher, or did use

9. *Merely*] entirely.
10. *passions of some difference*] conflicting passions or emotions.
11. *soil*] blemish.
12. *By means whereof*] in consequence of which misapprehension.
13. *shadow*] image.
14. *jealous on*] suspicious of.

To stale[15] with ordinary oaths my love
To every new protester; if you know
That I do fawn on men and hug them hard,
And after scandal[16] them; or if you know
That I profess myself[17] in banqueting
To all the rout, then hold me dangerous. [*Flourish and shout.*]

BRU. What means this shouting? I do fear, the people
Choose Caesar for their king.

CAS. Ay, do you fear it?
Then must I think you would not have it so.

BRU. I would not, Cassius, yet I love him well.
But wherefore do you hold me here so long?
What is it that you would impart to me?
If it be aught toward the general good,
Set honour in one eye and death i' the other,
And I will look on both indifferently:[18]
For let the gods so speed[19] me as I love
The name of honour more than I fear death.

CAS. I know that virtue to be in you, Brutus,
As well as I do know your outward favour.[20]
Well, honour is the subject of my story.
I cannot tell what you and other men
Think of this life, but, for my single self,
I had as lief not be as live to be
In awe of such a thing as I myself.
I was born free as Caesar; so were you:
We both have fed as well, and we can both
Endure the winter's cold as well as he:
For once, upon a raw and gusty day,
The troubled Tiber chafing with her shores,
Caesar said to me "Darest thou, Cassius, now
Leap in with me into this angry flood,
And swim to yonder point?" Upon the word,
Accoutred as I was, I plunged in
And bade him follow: so indeed he did.
The torrent roar'd, and we did buffet it

15. *To stale*] to vulgarize, make stale.
16. *scandal*] slander.
17. *profess myself*] make professions of friendship.
18. *indifferently*] with impartiality.
19. *speed*] favor.
20. *outward favour*] external features, countenance.

With lusty sinews, throwing it aside
And stemming it with hearts of controversy;[21]
But ere we could arrive the point proposed,
Caesar cried "Help me, Cassius, or I sink!"
I, as Aeneas our great ancestor
Did from the flames of Troy upon his shoulder
The old Anchises bear, so from the waves of Tiber
Did I the tired Caesar: and this man
Is now become a god, and Cassius is
A wretched creature, and must bend his body
If Caesar carelessly but nod on him.
He had a fever when he was in Spain,
And when the fit was on him, I did mark
How he did shake: 't is true, this god did shake;
His coward lips did from their colour fly,[22]
And that same eye whose bend[23] doth awe the world
Did lose his lustre: I did hear him groan:
Ay, and that tongue of his that bade the Romans
Mark him and write his speeches in their books,
Alas, it cried, "Give me some drink, Titinius,"
As a sick girl. Ye gods! it doth amaze me
A man of such a feeble temper[24] should
So get the start of[25] the majestic world
And bear the palm alone. [*Shout. Flourish.*]

BRU. Another general shout!
I do believe that these applauses are
For some new honours that are heap'd on Caesar.

CAS. Why, man, he doth bestride the narrow world
Like a Colossus,[26] and we petty men
Walk under his huge legs and peep about
To find ourselves dishonourable graves.
Men at some time are masters of their fates:
The fault, dear Brutus, is not in our stars,
But in ourselves, that we are underlings.

21. *hearts of controversy*] hearts bent on contest.
22. *His coward lips . . . fly*] The figure is that of a cowardly soldier running away from his colors or flag.
23. *bend*] glance.
24. *temper*] temperament, constitution.
25. *get the start of*] outstrip.
26. *Colossus*] the bronze statue of a man, 120 feet high, whose legs were so fixed in the harbor of Rhodes that ships sailed between them.

Brutus, and Caesar: what should be in that Caesar?
Why should that name be sounded more than yours?
Write them together, yours is as fair a name;
Sound them, it doth become the mouth as well;
Weigh them, it is as heavy; conjure with 'em,
Brutus will start a spirit as soon as Caesar.
Now, in the names of all the gods at once,
Upon what meat doth this our Caesar feed,
That he is grown so great? Age, thou art shamed!
Rome, thou hast lost the breed of noble bloods!
When went there by an age, since the great flood,
But it was famed with more than with one man?
When could they say till now that talk'd of Rome
That her wide walls encompass'd but one man?
Now is it Rome indeed, and room[27] enough,
When there is in it but one only man.
O, you and I have heard our fathers say
There was a Brutus[28] once that would have brook'd
The eternal devil to keep his state in Rome
As easily as a king.

BRU. That you do love me, I am nothing jealous;
What you would work me to, I have some aim:[29]
How I have thought of this and of these times,
I shall recount hereafter; for this present,
I would not, so with love I might entreat you,
Be any further moved. What you have said
I will consider; what you have to say
I will with patience hear, and find a time
Both meet to hear and answer such high things.
Till then, my noble friend, chew[30] upon this:
Brutus had rather be a villager
Than to repute himself a son of Rome
Under these hard conditions as this time
Is like to lay upon us.

CAS. I am glad that my weak words
Have struck but this much show of fire from Brutus.

BRU. The games are done, and Caesar is returning.

CAS. As they pass by, pluck Casca by the sleeve;

27. *Rome . . . room*] "Rome" was commonly pronounced like "room."
28. *Brutus*] Lucius Junius Brutus, the legendary founder of the Roman Republic, 509 B.C.
29. *aim*] inkling.
30. *chew*] reflect.

And he will, after his sour fashion, tell you
What hath proceeded worthy note to-day.

Re-enter CAESAR *and his Train.*

BRU. I will do so: but, look you, Cassius,
The angry spot doth glow on Caesar's brow,
And all the rest look like a chidden train:[31]
Calpurnia's cheek is pale, and Cicero
Looks with such ferret and such fiery eyes
As we have seen him in the Capitol,
Being cross'd in conference by some senators.
CAS. Casca will tell us what the matter is.
CAES. Antonius!
ANT. Caesar?
CAES. Let me have men about me that are fat,
Sleek-headed men, and such as sleep o' nights:
Yond Cassius has a lean and hungry look;
He thinks too much: such men are dangerous.
ANT. Fear him not, Caesar; he's not dangerous;
He is a noble Roman, and well given.[32]
CAES. Would he were fatter! but I fear him not:
Yet if my name were liable to fear,
I do not know the man I should avoid
So soon as that spare Cassius. He reads much;
He is a great observer, and he looks
Quite through the deeds of men: he loves no plays,
As thou dost, Antony; he hears no music:
Seldom he smiles, and smiles in such a sort
As if he mock'd himself, and scorn'd his spirit
That could be moved to smile at any thing.
Such men as he be never at heart's ease
Whiles they behold a greater than themselves,
And therefore are they very dangerous.
I rather tell thee what is to be fear'd
Than what I fear; for always I am Caesar.
Come on my right hand, for this ear is deaf,
And tell me truly what thou think'st of him.
[*Sennet. Exeunt* CAESAR *and all his Train but* CASCA.]
CASCA. You pull'd me by the cloak; would you speak with me?
BRU. Ay, Casca; tell us what hath chanced to-day,

31. *a chidden train*] a retinue of attendants who have been scolded.
32. *well given*] well-disposed.

That Caesar looks so sad.[33]

CASCA. Why, you were with him, were you not?

BRU. I should not then ask Casca what had chanced.

CASCA. Why, there was a crown offered him: and being offered him, he put it by with the back of his hand, thus: and then the people fell a-shouting.

BRU. What was the second noise for?

CASCA. Why, for that too.

CAS. They shouted thrice: what was the last cry for?

CASCA. Why, for that too.

BRU. Was the crown offered him thrice?

CASCA. Ay, marry, was't, and he put it by thrice, every time gentler than other; and at every putting by mine honest neighbours shouted.

CAS. Who offered him the crown?

CASCA. Why, Antony.

BRU. Tell us the manner of it, gentle Casca.

CASCA. I can as well be hang'd as tell the manner of it: it was mere foolery; I did not mark it. I saw Mark Antony offer him a crown: yet 't was not a crown neither, 't was one of these coronets: and, as I told you, he put it by once: but for all that, to my thinking, he would fain have had it. Then he offered it to him again; then he put it by again: but, to my thinking, he was very loath to lay his fingers off it. And then he offered it the third time; he put it the third time by: and still as he refused it, the rabblement hooted and clapped their chopped[34] hands and threw up their sweaty night-caps and uttered such a deal of stinking breath because Caesar refused the crown, that it had almost choked Caesar; for he swounded[35] and fell down at it: and for mine own part, I durst not laugh, for fear of opening my lips and receiving the bad air.

CAS. But, soft, I pray you: what, did Caesar swound?

CASCA. He fell down in the market-place and foamed at mouth and was speechless.

BRU. 'T is very like: he hath the falling-sickness.[36]

CAS. No, Caesar hath it not: but you, and I,
And honest Casca, we have the falling-sickness.

33. *sad*] serious.
34. *chopped*] chapped, disfigured with wrinkles.
35. *swounded*] fainted.
36. *falling-sickness*] epilepsy.

CASCA. I know not what you mean by that, but I am sure Caesar fell down. If the tag-rag people[37] did not clap him and hiss him according as he pleased and displeased them, as they use to do the players in the theatre, I am no true man.

BRU. What said he when he came unto himself?

CASCA. Marry, before he fell down, when he perceived the common herd was glad he refused the crown, he plucked me ope[38] his doublet and offered them his throat to cut. An I had been a man of any occupation,[39] if I would not have taken him at a word, I would I might go to hell among the rogues. And so he fell. When he came to himself again, he said, if he had done or said any thing amiss, he desired their worships to think it was his infirmity. Three or four wenches, where I stood, cried "Alas, good soul!" and forgave him with all their hearts: but there's no heed to be taken of them; if Caesar had stabbed their mothers, they would have done no less.

BRU. And after that, he came, thus sad, away?

CASCA. Ay.

CAS. Did Cicero say any thing?

CASCA. Ay, he spoke Greek.

CAS. To what effect?

CASCA. Nay, an I tell you that, I'll ne'er look you i' the face again: but those that understood him smiled at one another and shook their heads; but for mine own part, it was Greek to me. I could tell you more news too: Marullus and Flavius, for pulling scarfs off Caesar's images, are put to silence.[40] Fare you well. There was more foolery yet, if I could remember it.

CAS. Will you sup with me to-night, Casca?

CASCA. No, I am promised forth.[41]

CAS. Will you dine with me to-morrow?

CASCA. Ay, if I be alive, and your mind hold,[42] and your dinner worth the eating.

CAS. Good; I will expect you.

CASCA. Do so: farewell, both. [*Exit.*]

BRU. What a blunt fellow is this grown to be!
He was quick mettle when he went to school.

37. *tag-rag people*] rabble.
38. *me ope*] open.
39. *a man of any occupation*] a workman, a man of action.
40. *put to silence*] dismissed or executed.
41. *promised forth*] already engaged.
42. *and your mind hold*] and you still wish me to come.

CAS. So is he now in execution
Of any bold or noble enterprise,
However he puts on this tardy form.
This rudeness is a sauce to his good wit,
Which gives men stomach to digest his words
With better appetite.

BRU. And so it is. For this time I will leave you:
To-morrow, if you please to speak with me,
I will come home to you, or, if you will,
Come home to me and I will wait for you.

CAS. I will do so: till then, think of the world. [*Exit* BRUTUS.]
Well, Brutus, thou art noble; yet, I see,
Thy honourable metal may be wrought
From that it is disposed:[43] therefore it is meet
That noble minds keep ever with their likes;
For who so firm that cannot be seduced?
Caesar doth bear me hard;[44] but he loves Brutus:
If I were Brutus now and he were Cassius,
He should not humour me. I will this night,
In several hands,[45] in at his windows throw,
As if they came from several citizens,
Writings, all tending to the great opinion
That Rome holds of his name, wherein obscurely
Caesar's ambition shall be glanced at:[46]
And after this let Caesar seat him sure;
For we will shake him, or worse days endure. [*Exit.*]

Scene III—A street

Thunder and lightning. Enter, from opposite sides, CASCA, *with his sword drawn, and* CICERO.

CIC. Good even, Casca: brought you Caesar home?
Why are you breathless? and why stare you so?

43. *From that it is disposed*] from its natural disposition.
44. *bear me hard*] have a grudge against me.
45. *hands*] handwritings.
46. *glanced at*] hinted at, censured.

CASCA. Are you not moved, when all the sway[1] of earth
Shakes like a thing unfirm? O Cicero,
I have seen tempests, when the scolding winds
Have rived the knotty oaks, and I have seen
The ambitious ocean swell and rage and foam,
To be exalted with the threatening clouds;
But never till to-night, never till now,
Did I go through a tempest dropping fire.
Either there is a civil strife in heaven,
Or else the world too saucy with the gods
Incenses them to send destruction.

CIC. Why, saw you any thing more wonderful?

CASCA. A common slave—you know him well by sight—
Held up his left hand, which did flame and burn
Like twenty torches join'd, and yet his hand
Not sensible of fire remain'd unscorch'd.
Besides—I ha' not since put up my sword—
Against the Capitol I met a lion,
Who glazed[2] upon me and went surly by
Without annoying me: and there were drawn
Upon a heap[3] a hundred ghastly women
Transformed with their fear, who swore they saw
Men all in fire walk up and down the streets.
And yesterday the bird of night[4] did sit
Even at noon-day upon the market-place,
Hooting and shrieking. When these prodigies[5]
Do so conjointly meet, let not men say
"These are their reasons: they are natural:"
For, I believe, they are portentous things
Unto the climate[6] that they point upon.

CIC. Indeed, it is a strange-disposed time:
But men may construe things after their fashion,
Clean from[7] the purpose of the things themselves.
Comes Caesar to the Capitol to-morrow?

CASCA. He doth; for he did bid Antonius
Send word to you he would be there to-morrow.

1. *sway*] constitution.
2. *glazed*] stared.
3. *drawn Upon a heap*] collected into a crowd.
4. *the bird of night*] the owl.
5. *prodigies*] omens.
6. *climate*] region.
7. *Clean from*] contrary to.

CIC. Good night then, Casca: this disturbed sky
Is not to walk in.
CASCA. Farewell, Cicero. [*Exit* CICERO.]

Enter CASSIUS.

CAS. Who's there?
CASCA. A Roman.
CAS. Casca, by your voice.
CASCA. Your ear is good. Cassius, what night is this!
CAS. A very pleasing night to honest men.
CASCA. Who ever knew the heavens menace so?
CAS. Those that have known the earth so full of faults.
For my part, I have walk'd about the streets,
Submitting me unto the perilous night,
And thus unbraced,[8] Casca, as you see,
Have bared my bosom to the thunder-stone;[9]
And when the cross[10] blue lightning seem'd to open
The breast of heaven, I did present myself
Even in the aim and very flash of it.
CASCA. But wherefore did you so much tempt the heavens?
It is the part of men to fear and tremble
When the most mighty gods by tokens send
Such dreadful heralds to astonish us.
CAS. You are dull, Casca, and those sparks of life
That should be in a Roman you do want,
Or else you use not. You look pale and gaze
And put on fear and cast yourself in wonder,
To see the strange impatience of the heavens:
But if you would consider the true cause
Why all these fires, why all these gliding ghosts,
Why birds and beasts from quality and kind,[11]
Why old men fool and children calculate,[12]
Why all these things change from their ordinance,
Their natures and preformed faculties,
To monstrous quality, why, you shall find
That heaven hath infused them with these spirits
To make them instruments of fear and warning

8. *unbraced*] with doublet unbuttoned.
9. *thunder-stone*] thunderbolt.
10. *cross*] forked.
11. *from quality and kind*] contrary to disposition and nature.
12. *calculate*] foretell.

Unto some monstrous state.
Now could I, Casca, name to thee a man
Most like this dreadful night,
That thunders, lightens, opens graves, and roars
As doth the lion in the Capitol,
A man no mightier than thyself or me
In personal action, yet prodigious[13] grown
And fearful,[14] as these strange eruptions are.

CASCA. 'T is Caesar that you mean; is it not, Cassius?

CAS. Let it be who it is: for Romans now
Have thews[15] and limbs like to their ancestors;
But, woe the while! our fathers' minds are dead,
And we are govern'd with our mothers' spirits;
Our yoke and sufferance show us womanish.

CASCA. Indeed they say the senators to-morrow
Mean to establish Caesar as a king;
And he shall wear his crown by sea and land,
In every place save here in Italy.

CAS. I know where I will wear this dagger then:
Cassius from bondage will deliver Cassius.
Therein, ye gods, you make the weak most strong;
Therein, ye gods, you tyrants do defeat:
Nor stony tower, nor walls of beaten brass,
Nor airless dungeon, nor strong links of iron,
Can be retentive to[16] the strength of spirit;
But life, being weary of these worldly bars,
Never lacks power to dismiss itself.
If I know this, know all the world besides,
That part of tyranny that I do bear
I can shake off at pleasure. [*Thunder still.*]

CASCA. So can I:
So every bondman in his own hand bears
The power to cancel his captivity.

CAS. And why should Caesar be a tyrant then?
Poor man! I know he would not be a wolf
But that he sees the Romans are but sheep:
He were no lion, were not Romans hinds.

13. *prodigious*] portentous.
14. *fearful*] causing fear.
15. *thews*] sinews.
16. *be retentive to*] hold in or repress.

Those that with haste will make a mighty fire
Begin it with weak straws: what trash is Rome,
What rubbish and what offal, when it serves
For the base matter to illuminate
So vile a thing as Caesar! But, O grief,
Where hast thou led me? I perhaps speak this
Before a willing bondman; then I know
My answer must be made.[17] But I am arm'd,
And dangers are to me indifferent.

CASCA. You speak to Casca, and to such a man
That is no fleering[18] tell-tale. Hold, my hand:
Be factious[19] for redress of all these griefs,
And I will set this foot of mine as far
As who goes farthest.

CAS. There's a bargain made.
Now know you, Casca, I have moved already
Some certain of the noblest-minded Romans
To undergo with me an enterprise
Of honourable-dangerous consequence;
And I do know, by this they stay for me
In Pompey's porch:[20] for now, this fearful night,
There is no stir or walking in the streets,
And the complexion of the element
In favour's like[21] the work we have in hand,
Most bloody, fiery, and most terrible.

Enter CINNA.

CASCA. Stand close[22] a while, for here comes one in haste.

CAS. 'T is Cinna; I do know him by his gait;
He is a friend. Cinna, where haste you so?

CIN. To find out you. Who's that? Metellus Cimber?

CAS. No, it is Casca; one incorporate
To our attempts. Am I not stay'd for, Cinna?

CIN. I am glad on't. What a fearful night is this!
There's two or three of us have seen strange sights.

17. *My answer must be made*] I must answer (to Caesar) for my outspokenness.
18. *fleering*] fawning.
19. *Be factious*] form a party or faction.
20. *Pompey's porch*] a spacious portico outside the theater built by Pompey in the Campus Martius.
21. *In favour's like*] resembles.
22. *Stand close*] keep concealed.

CAS. Am I not stay'd for? tell me.
CIN. Yes, you are.
O Cassius, if you could
But win the noble Brutus to our party—
CAS. Be you content: good Cinna, take this paper,
And look you lay it in the praetor's chair,
Where Brutus may but find it, and throw this
In at his window; set this up with wax
Upon old Brutus' statue:[23] all this done,
Repair to Pompey's porch, where you shall find us.
Is Decius Brutus and Trebonius there?
CIN. All but Metellus Cimber; and he's gone
To seek you at your house. Well, I will hie,
And so bestow these papers as you bade me.
CAS. That done, repair to Pompey's theatre. [*Exit* CINNA.]
Come, Casca, you and I will yet ere day
See Brutus at his house: three parts of him
Is ours already, and the man entire
Upon the next encounter yields him ours.
CASCA. O, he sits high in all the people's hearts;
And that which would appear offence in us
His countenance, like richest alchemy,
Will change to virtue and to worthiness.
CAS. Him and his worth and our great need of him
You have right well conceited.[24] Let us go,
For it is after midnight, and ere day
We will awake him and be sure of him. [*Exeunt*.]

23. *old Brutus' statue*] the statue of Lucius Junius Brutus.
24. *conceited*] conceived, imagined.

Act II—Scene I—Rome

BRUTUS'S ORCHARD

Enter BRUTUS.

BRU. What, Lucius, ho!
I cannot, by the progress of the stars,
Give guess how near to day. Lucius, I say!
I would it were my fault to sleep so soundly.
When, Lucius, when? awake, I say! what, Lucius!

Enter LUCIUS.

LUC. Call'd you, my lord?
BRU. Get me a taper in my study, Lucius:
When it is lighted, come and call me here.
LUC. I will, my lord. [*Exit.*]
BRU. It must be by his death: and, for my part,
I know no personal cause to spurn at him,
But for the general.[1] He would be crown'd:
How that might change his nature, there's the question:
It is the bright day that brings forth the adder;
And that craves wary walking. Crown him?—that;—
And then, I grant, we put a sting in him,
That at his will he may do danger with.
The abuse of greatness is when it disjoins
Remorse[2] from power: and, to speak truth of Caesar,
I have not known when his affections sway'd[3]

1. *for the general*] in the interest of the public.
2. *Remorse*] consideration for others, pity.
3. *sway'd*] ruled.

More than his reason. But 't is a common proof,[4]
That lowliness is young ambition's ladder,
Whereto the climber-upward turns his face;
But when he once attains the upmost round,
He then unto the ladder turns his back,
Looks in the clouds, scorning the base degrees
By which he did ascend: so Caesar may;
Then, lest he may, prevent. And, since the quarrel
Will bear no colour for the thing he is,[5]
Fashion it thus; that what he is, augmented,
Would run to these and these extremities:
And therefore think him as a serpent's egg
Which hatch'd would as his kind grow mischievous,
And kill him in the shell.

Re-enter LUCIUS.

LUC. The taper burneth in your closet, sir.
Searching the window for a flint I found
This paper thus seal'd up, and I am sure
It did not lie there when I went to bed. [*Gives him the letter.*]
BRU. Get you to bed again; it is not day.
Is not to-morrow, boy, the ides of March?
LUC. I know not, sir.
BRU. Look in the calendar and bring me word.
LUC. I will, sir. [*Exit.*]
BRU. The exhalations[6] whizzing in the air
Give so much light that I may read by them.
[*Opens the letter and reads.*]

"Brutus, thou sleep'st: awake and see thyself.
Shall Rome, &c. Speak, strike, redress.
Brutus, thou sleep'st: awake."

Such instigations have been often dropp'd
Where I have took them up.
"Shall Rome, &c." Thus must I piece it out:
Shall Rome stand under one man's awe? What, Rome?
My ancestors did from the streets of Rome

4. *proof*] fact, experience.
5. *since the quarrel . . . he is*] since there is no possible pretext for quarreling with Caesar on the ground of anything he is by nature (or has yet done).
6. *exhalations*] meteors.

The Tarquin drive, when he was call'd a king.
"Speak, strike, redress." Am I entreated
To speak and strike? O Rome, I make thee promise,
If the redress will follow, thou receivest
Thy full petition at the hand of Brutus!

Re-enter LUCIUS.

LUC. Sir, March is wasted fifteen days. [*Knocking within.*]
BRU. 'T is good. Go to the gate; somebody knocks. [*Exit* LUCIUS.]
Since Cassius first did whet me against Caesar
I have not slept.
Between the acting of a dreadful thing
And the first motion,[7] all the interim is
Like a phantasma or a hideous dream:
The Genius[8] and the mortal instruments[9]
Are then in council, and the state of man,
Like to a little kingdom, suffers then
The nature of an insurrection.

Re-enter LUCIUS.

LUC. Sir, 't is your brother[10] Cassius at the door,
Who doth desire to see you.
BRU. Is he alone?
LUC. No, sir; there are moe[11] with him.
BRU. Do you know them?
LUC. No, sir; their hats are pluck'd about their ears,
And half their faces buried in their cloaks,
That by no means I may discover them
By any mark of favour.[12]
BRU. Let 'em enter. [*Exit* LUCIUS.]
They are the faction. O conspiracy,
Shamest thou to show thy dangerous brow by night,
When evils are most free? O, then, by day
Where wilt thou find a cavern dark enough

7. *motion*] impulse, prompting.
8. *Genius*] soul.
9. *mortal instruments*] agents of reason and will.
10. *brother*] brother-in-law. Cassius had married Brutus's sister Junia.
11. *moe*] more.
12. *favour*] feature.

To mask thy monstrous visage? Seek none, conspiracy;
Hide it in smiles and affability:
For if thou path,[13] thy native semblance on,
Not Erebus[14] itself were dim enough
To hide thee from prevention.

Enter the conspirators, CASSIUS, CASCA, DECIUS, CINNA, METELLUS CIMBER, *and* TREBONIUS.

CAS. I think we are too bold upon your rest:
Good morrow, Brutus; do we trouble you?
BRU. I have been up this hour, awake all night.
Know I these men that come along with you?
CAS. Yes, every man of them; and no man here
But honours you; and every one doth wish
You had but that opinion of yourself
Which every noble Roman bears of you.
This is Trebonius.
BRU. He is welcome hither.
CAS. This, Decius Brutus.
BRU. He is welcome too.
CAS. This, Casca; this, Cinna; and this, Metellus Cimber.
BRU. They are all welcome.
What watchful cares do interpose themselves
Betwixt your eyes and night?
CAS. Shall I entreat a word? [*They whisper.*]
DEC. Here lies the east: doth not the day break here?
CASCA. No.
CIN. O, pardon, sir, it doth, and yon grey lines
That fret the clouds are messengers of day.
CASCA. You shall confess that you are both deceived.
Here, as I point my sword, the sun arises;
Which is a great way growing on[15] the south,
Weighing[16] the youthful season of the year.
Some two months hence up higher toward the north
He first presents his fire, and the high east
Stands as the Capitol, directly here.

13. *path*] proceed.
14. *Erebus*] a dark region between earth and Hades.
15. *growing on*] toward.
16. *Weighing*] considering.

BRU. Give me your hands all over,[17] one by one.
CAS. And let us swear our resolution.
BRU. No, not an oath: if not the face of men,
The sufferance of our souls, the time's abuse,—[18]
If these be motives weak, break off betimes,
And every man hence to his idle bed;
So let high-sighted[19] tyranny range on
Till each man drop by lottery.[20] But if these,
As I am sure they do, bear fire enough
To kindle cowards and to steel with valour
The melting spirits of women, then, countrymen,
What need we any spur but our own cause
To prick[21] us to redress? what other bond
Than secret Romans that have spoke the word,
And will not palter?[22] and what other oath
Than honesty to honesty engaged
That this shall be or we will fall for it?
Swear priests and cowards and men cautelous,[23]
Old feeble carrions[24] and such suffering souls
That welcome wrongs; unto bad causes swear
Such creatures as men doubt: but do not stain
The even virtue of our enterprise,
Nor the insuppressive[25] mettle of our spirits,
To think that or our cause or our performance
Did need an oath; when every drop of blood
That every Roman bears, and nobly bears,
Is guilty of a several bastardy[26]
If he do break the smallest particle
Of any promise that hath pass'd from him.
CAS. But what of Cicero? shall we sound him?
I think he will stand very strong with us.
CASCA. Let us not leave him out.
CIN. No, by no means.

17. *all over*] all in succession.
18. *the time's abuse*] the wrongs or grievances of the age.
19. *high-sighted*] haughty.
20. *by lottery*] by compulsorily drawing lots.
21. *prick*] spur.
22. *palter*] equivocate.
23. *cautelous*] deceitful.
24. *carrions*] corpses (a common word of contempt).
25. *insuppressive*] insuppressible.
26. *a several bastardy*] a separate, distinct act of treachery.

MET. O, let us have him, for his silver hairs
Will purchase us a good opinion,
And buy men's voices to commend our deeds:
It shall be said his judgement ruled our hands;
Our youths and wildness shall no whit appear,
But all be buried in his gravity.
BRU. O, name him not: let us not break[27] with him,
For he will never follow any thing
That other men begin.
CAS. Then leave him out.
CASCA. Indeed he is not fit.
DEC. Shall no man else be touch'd but only Caesar?
CAS. Decius, well urged: I think it is not meet
Mark Antony, so well beloved of Caesar,
Should outlive Caesar: we shall find of him
A shrewd contriver; and you know his means,
If he improve them, may well stretch so far
As to annoy[28] us all: which to prevent,
Let Antony and Caesar fall together.
BRU. Our course will seem too bloody, Caius Cassius,
To cut the head off and then hack the limbs,
Like wrath in death and envy[29] afterwards;
For Antony is but a limb of Caesar:
Let us be sacrificers, but not butchers, Caius.
We all stand up against the spirit of Caesar,
And in the spirit of men there is no blood:
O, that we then could come by Caesar's spirit,
And not dismember Caesar! But, alas,
Caesar must bleed for it! And, gentle friends,
Let's kill him boldly, but not wrathfully;
Let's carve him as a dish fit for the gods,
Not hew him as a carcass fit for hounds:
And let our hearts, as subtle masters do,
Stir up their servants to an act of rage
And after seem to chide 'em. This shall make
Our purpose necessary and not envious:[30]
Which so appearing to the common eyes,
We shall be call'd purgers, not murderers.

27. *break*] communicate.
28. *annoy*] harm.
29. *envy*] malice.
30. *envious*] malicious.

And for Mark Antony, think not of him;
For he can do no more than Caesar's arm
When Caesar's head is off.

CAS. Yet I fear him,
For in the ingrafted love he bears to Caesar—

BRU. Alas, good Cassius, do not think of him:
If he love Caesar, all that he can do
Is to himself, take thought[31] and die for Caesar:
And that were much he should,[32] for he is given
To sports, to wildness and much company.

TREB. There is no fear[33] in him; let him not die;
For he will live and laugh at this hereafter. [*Clock strikes.*]

BRU. Peace! count the clock.

CAS. The clock hath stricken three.

TREB. 'T is time to part.

CAS. But it is doubtful yet
Whether Caesar will come forth to-day or no;
For he is superstitious grown of late,
Quite from the main opinion[34] he held once
Of fantasy, of dreams and ceremonies:[35]
It may be these apparent prodigies,
The unaccustom'd terror of this night
And the persuasion of his augurers,
May hold him from the Capitol to-day.

DEC. Never fear that: if he be so resolved,
I can o'ersway him; for he loves to hear
That unicorns may be betray'd with trees
And bears with glasses,[36] elephants with holes,
Lions with toils[37] and men with flatterers:
But when I tell him he hates flatterers,
He says he does, being then most flattered.
Let me work;
For I can give his humour the true bent,
And I will bring him to the Capitol.

31. *take thought*] grieve.
32. *that were much he should*] that would be difficult for him.
33. *no fear*] nothing to fear.
34. *from the main opinion*] contrary to the firm opinion.
35. *ceremonies*] omens.
36. *glasses*] mirrors.
37. *toils*] nets.

CAS. Nay, we will all of us be there to fetch him.
BRU. By the eighth hour: is that the uttermost?[38]
CIN. Be that the uttermost, and fail not then.
MET. Caius Ligarius doth bear Caesar hard,
Who rated him for speaking well of Pompey:
I wonder none of you have thought of him.
BRU. Now, good Metellus, go along by him:
He loves me well, and I have given him reasons;
Send him but hither, and I'll fashion him.
CAS. The morning comes upon 's: we'll leave you, Brutus:
And, friends, disperse yourselves: but all remember
What you have said and show yourselves true Romans.
BRU. Good gentlemen, look fresh and merrily;
Let not our looks put on[39] our purposes;
But bear it as our Roman actors do,
With untired spirits and formal constancy:[40]
And so, good morrow to you every one. [*Exeunt all but* BRUTUS.]
Boy! Lucius! Fast asleep! It is no matter;
Enjoy the honey-heavy dew of slumber:
Thou hast no figures[41] nor no fantasies,
Which busy care draws in the brains of men;
Therefore thou sleep'st so sound.

Enter PORTIA.

POR. Brutus, my lord!
BRU. Portia, what mean you? wherefore rise you now?
It is not for your health thus to commit
Your weak condition to the raw cold morning.
POR. Nor for yours neither. You've ungently, Brutus,
Stole from my bed: and yesternight at supper
You suddenly arose and walk'd about,
Musing and sighing, with your arms across;
And when I ask'd you what the matter was,
You stared upon me with ungentle looks:
I urged you further; then you scratch'd your head,
And too impatiently stamp'd with your foot:
Yet I insisted, yet you answer'd not,

38. *uttermost*] latest.
39. *put on*] reveal.
40. *formal constancy*] consistent dignity.
41. *figures*] vain fancies.

But with an angry wafture[42] of your hand
Gave sign for me to leave you: so I did,
Fearing to strengthen that impatience
Which seem'd too much enkindled, and withal
Hoping it was but an effect of humour,[43]
Which sometime hath his hour with every man.
It will not let you eat, nor talk, nor sleep,
And, could it work so much upon your shape
As it hath much prevail'd on your condition,[44]
I should not know you, Brutus. Dear my lord,
Make me acquainted with your cause of grief.

BRU. I am not well in health, and that is all.

POR. Brutus is wise, and, were he not in health,
He would embrace the means to come by it.

BRU. Why, so I do: good Portia, go to bed.

POR. Is Brutus sick, and is it physical[45]
To walk unbraced and suck up the humours
Of the dank morning? What, is Brutus sick,
And will he steal out of his wholesome bed,
To dare the vile contagion of the night,
And tempt the rheumy and unpurged[46] air
To add unto his sickness? No, my Brutus;
You have some sick offence[47] within your mind,
Which by the right and virtue of my place
I ought to know of: and, upon my knees,
I charm[48] you, by my once commended beauty,
By all your vows of love and that great vow
Which did incorporate and make us one,
That you unfold to me, yourself, your half,
Why you are heavy, and what men to-night
Have had resort to you; for here have been
Some six or seven, who did hide their faces
Even from darkness.

BRU. Kneel not, gentle Portia.

POR. I should not need, if you were gentle Brutus.

42. *wafture*] wave.
43. *humour*] caprice.
44. *condition*] disposition.
45. *physical*] wholesome.
46. *rheumy and unpurged*] damp and impure.
47. *sick offence*] morbid obstruction.
48. *charm*] adjure.

Within the bond of marriage, tell me, Brutus,
Is it excepted I should know no secrets
That appertain to you? Am I yourself
But, as it were, in sort or limitation,
To keep with you at meals, comfort your bed,
And talk to you sometimes? Dwell I but in the suburbs
Of your good pleasure? If it be no more,
Portia is Brutus' harlot, not his wife.

BRU. You are my true and honourable wife,
As dear to me as are the ruddy drops
That visit my sad heart.

POR. If this were true, then should I know this secret.
I grant I am a woman, but withal
A woman that Lord Brutus took to wife:
I grant I am a woman, but withal
A woman well reputed, Cato's daughter.
Think you I am no stronger than my sex,
Being so father'd and so husbanded?
Tell me your counsels, I will not disclose 'em:
I have made strong proof of my constancy,
Giving myself a voluntary wound
Here in the thigh: can I bear that with patience
And not my husband's secrets?

BRU. O ye gods,
Render me worthy of this noble wife! [*Knocking within.*]
Hark, hark! one knocks: Portia, go in a while;
And by and by thy bosom shall partake
The secrets of my heart:
All my engagements I will construe to thee,
All the charactery[49] of my sad brows.
Leave me with haste. [*Exit* PORTIA.] Lucius, who's that knocks?

Re-enter LUCIUS *with* LIGARIUS.

LUC. Here is a sick man that would speak with you.

BRU. Caius Ligarius, that Metellus spake of.
Boy, stand aside. Caius Ligarius! how?

LIG. Vouchsafe[50] good morrow from a feeble tongue.

BRU. O, what a time have you chose out, brave Caius,

49. *charactery*] written symbols.
50. *Vouchsafe*] deign to accept.

To wear a kerchief![51] Would you were not sick!
LIG. I am not sick, if Brutus have in hand
Any exploit worthy the name of honour.
BRU. Such an exploit have I in hand, Ligarius,
Had you a healthful ear to hear of it.
LIG. By all the gods that Romans bow before,
I here discard my sickness! Soul of Rome!
Brave son, derived from honourable loins!
Thou, like an exorcist,[52] hast conjured up
My mortified[53] spirit. Now bid me run,
And I will strive with things impossible,
Yea, get the better of them. What's to do?
BRU. A piece of work that will make sick men whole.
LIG. But are not some whole that we must make sick?
BRU. That must we also. What it is, my Caius,
I shall unfold to thee, as we are going
To whom it must be done.
LIG. Set on your foot,
And with a heart new-fired I follow you,
To do I know not what: but it sufficeth
That Brutus leads me on.
BRU. Follow me then. [*Exeunt.*]

Scene II—Caesar's house

Thunder and lightning. Enter CAESAR, *in his night-gown.*

CAES. Nor heaven nor earth have been at peace to-night:
Thrice hath Calpurnia in her sleep cried out,
"Help, ho! they murder Caesar!" Who's within?

Enter a Servant.

SERV. My lord?
CAES. Go bid the priests do present sacrifice,
And bring me their opinions of success.[1]

51. *To wear a kerchief*] a common mode of treating illness.
52. *exorcist*] one who raises spirits.
53. *mortified*] dead.

1. *success*] the result.

SERV. I will, my lord. [*Exit.*]

Enter CALPURNIA.

CAL. What mean you, Caesar? think you to walk forth?
You shall not stir out of your house to-day.
CAES. Caesar shall forth: the things that threaten'd me
Ne'er look'd but on my back; when they shall see
The face of Caesar, they are vanished.
CAL. Caesar, I never stood on ceremonies,[2]
Yet now they fright me. There is one within,
Besides the things that we have heard and seen,
Recounts most horrid sights seen by the watch.
A lioness hath whelped in the streets;
And graves have yawn'd, and yielded up their dead;
Fierce fiery warriors fight upon the clouds,
In ranks and squadrons and right form of war,
Which drizzled blood upon the Capitol;
The noise of battle hurtled in the air,
Horses did neigh and dying men did groan,
And ghosts did shriek and squeal about the streets.
O Caesar! these things are beyond all use,
And I do fear them.
CAES. What can be avoided
Whose end is purposed by the mighty gods?
Yet Caesar shall go forth; for these predictions
Are to the world in general as to Caesar.
CAL. When beggars die, there are no comets seen;
The heavens themselves blaze forth the death of princes.
CAES. Cowards die many times before their deaths;
The valiant never taste of death but once.
Of all the wonders that I yet have heard,
It seems to me most strange that men should fear;
Seeing that death, a necessary end,
Will come when it will come.

Re-enter Servant.

What say the augurers?
SERV. They would not have you to stir forth to-day.
Plucking the entrails of an offering forth,
They could not find a heart within the beast.
CAES. The gods do this in shame of cowardice:

2. *stood on ceremonies*] attached importance to omens.

Caesar should be a beast without a heart
If he should stay at home to-day for fear.
No, Caesar shall not: danger knows full well
That Caesar is more dangerous than he:
We are two lions litter'd in one day,
And I the elder and more terrible:
And Caesar shall go forth.

CAL. Alas, my lord,
Your wisdom is consumed in confidence.
Do not go forth to-day: call it my fear
That keeps you in the house and not your own.
We'll send Mark Antony to the senate-house,
And he shall say you are not well to-day:
Let me, upon my knee, prevail in this.

CAES. Mark Antony shall say I am not well,
And, for thy humour, I will stay at home.

Enter DECIUS.

Here's Decius Brutus, he shall tell them so.

DEC. Caesar, all hail! good morrow, worthy Caesar:
I come to fetch you to the senate-house.

CAES. And you are come in very happy time,
To bear my greeting to the senators
And tell them that I will not come to-day:
Cannot, is false, and that I dare not, falser:
I will not come to-day: tell them so, Decius.

CAL. Say he is sick.

CAES. Shall Caesar send a lie?
Have I in conquest stretch'd mine arm so far,
To be afeard to tell graybeards the truth?
Decius, go tell them Caesar will not come.

DEC. Most mighty Caesar, let me know some cause,
Lest I be laugh'd at when I tell them so.

CAES. The cause is in my will: I will not come;
That is enough to satisfy the senate.
But, for your private satisfaction,
Because I love you, I will let you know.
Calpurnia here, my wife, stays me at home:
She dreamt to-night she saw my statue,
Which like a fountain with an hundred spouts
Did run pure blood, and many lusty Romans
Came smiling and did bathe their hands in it:

And these does she apply for warnings and portents
And evils imminent, and on her knee
Hath begg'd that I will stay at home to-day.

DEC. This dream is all amiss interpreted;
It was a vision fair and fortunate:
Your statue spouting blood in many pipes,
In which so many smiling Romans bathed,
Signifies that from you great Rome shall suck
Reviving blood, and that great men shall press
For tinctures,[3] stains, relics and cognizance.[4]
This by Calpurnia's dream is signified.

CAES. And this way have you well expounded it.

DEC. I have, when you have heard what I can say:
And know it now: the senate have concluded
To give this day a crown to mighty Caesar.
If you shall send them word you will not come,
Their minds may change. Besides, it were a mock[5]
Apt to be render'd,[6] for some one to say
"Break up the senate till another time,
When Caesar's wife shall meet with better dreams."
If Caesar hide himself, shall they not whisper
"Lo, Caesar is afraid"?
Pardon me, Caesar, for my dear dear love
To your proceeding[7] bids me tell you this,
And reason to my love is liable.[8]

CAES. How foolish do your fears seem now, Calpurnia!
I am ashamed I did yield to them.
Give me my robe, for I will go.

Enter PUBLIUS, BRUTUS, LIGARIUS, METELLUS, CASCA, TREBONIUS, *and* CINNA.

And look where Publius is come to fetch me.

PUB. Good morrow, Caesar.

CAES. Welcome, Publius.
What, Brutus, are you stirr'd so early too?
Good morrow, Casca. Caius Ligarius,

3. *tinctures*] handkerchiefs dipped in martyr's blood.
4. *cognizance*] memento.
5. *mock*] sarcasm.
6. *Apt to be render'd*] likely to be offered as a rejoinder.
7. *proceeding*] welfare, advancement.
8. *liable*] subject.

Caesar was ne'er so much your enemy
As that same ague which hath made you lean.
What is't o'clock?

BRU. Caesar, 't is strucken eight.

CAES. I thank you for your pains and courtesy.

Enter ANTONY.

See! Antony, that revels long o' nights,
Is notwithstanding up. Good morrow, Antony.

ANT. So to most noble Caesar.

CAES. Bid them prepare within:
I am to blame to be thus waited for.
Now, Cinna: now, Metellus: what, Trebonius!
I have an hour's talk in store for you;
Remember that you call on me to-day:
Be near me, that I may remember you.

TREB. Caesar, I will. [*Aside.*] And so near will I be,
That your best friends shall wish I had been further.

CAES. Good friends, go in and taste some wine with me;
And we like friends will straightway go together.

BRU. [*Aside.*] That every like is not the same, O Caesar,
The heart of Brutus yearns[9] to think upon! [*Exeunt.*]

Scene III—A street near the Capitol

Enter ARTEMIDORUS, *reading a paper.*

ART. "Caesar, beware of Brutus; take heed of Cassius; come not near Casca; have an eye to Cinna; trust not Trebonius; mark well Metellus Cimber; Decius Brutus loves thee not; thou hast wronged Caius Ligarius. There is but one mind in all these men, and it is bent against Caesar. If thou beest not immortal, look about you: security gives way to[1] conspiracy. The mighty gods defend thee!
Thy lover,[2] ARTEMIDORUS."

Here will I stand till Caesar pass along,

9. *yearns*] grieves.

1. *security gives way to*] overconfidence opens the road to.
2. *lover*] friend.

And as a suitor will I give him this.
My heart laments that virtue cannot live
Out of the teeth of emulation.[3]
If thou read this, O Caesar, thou mayst live;
If not, the Fates with traitors do contrive. [*Exit.*]

Scene IV—Another part of the same street, before the house of Brutus

Enter PORTIA *and* LUCIUS.

POR. I prithee, boy, run to the senate-house;
Stay not to answer me, but get thee gone.
Why dost thou stay?
LUC. To know my errand, madam.
POR. I would have had thee there, and here again,
Ere I can tell thee what thou shouldst do there.
O constancy, be strong upon my side!
Set a huge mountain 'tween my heart and tongue!
I have a man's mind, but a woman's might.
How hard it is for women to keep counsel!
Art thou here yet?
LUC. Madam, what should I do?
Run to the Capitol, and nothing else?
And so return to you, and nothing else?
POR. Yes, bring me word, boy, if thy lord look well,
For he went sickly forth: and take good note
What Caesar doth, what suitors press to him.
Hark, boy! what noise is that?
LUC. I hear none, madam.
POR. Prithee, listen well:
I heard a bustling rumour[1] like a fray,
And the wind brings it from the Capitol.
LUC. Sooth, madam, I hear nothing.

Enter the Soothsayer.

POR. Come hither, fellow: which way hast thou been?

3. *emulation*] malicious rivalry.

1. *rumour*] noise.

SOOTH. At mine own house, good lady.
POR. What is 't o'clock?
SOOTH. About the ninth hour, lady.
POR. Is Caesar yet gone to the Capitol?
SOOTH. Madam, not yet: I go to take my stand,
To see him pass on to the Capitol.
POR. Thou hast some suit to Caesar, hast thou not?
SOOTH. That I have, lady: if it will please Caesar
To be so good to Caesar as to hear me,
I shall beseech him to befriend himself.
POR. Why, know'st thou any harm's intended towards him?
SOOTH. None that I know will be, much that I fear may chance.
Good morrow to you. Here the street is narrow:
The throng that follows Caesar at the heels,
Of senators, of praetors, common suitors,
Will crowd a feeble man almost to death:
I'll get me to a place more void and there
Speak to great Caesar as he comes along. [*Exit.*]
POR. I must go in. Ay me, how weak a thing
The heart of woman is! O Brutus,
The heavens speed thee in thine enterprise!
Sure, the boy heard me. Brutus hath a suit
That Caesar will not grant. O, I grow faint.
Run, Lucius, and commend me to my lord;
Say I am merry: come to me again,
And bring me word what he doth say to thee. [*Exeunt severally.*]

Act III—Scene I—Rome

BEFORE THE CAPITOL—THE SENATE SITTING ABOVE

A *crowd of people; among them* ARTEMIDORUS *and the* Soothsayer. *Flourish. Enter* CAESAR, BRUTUS, CASSIUS, CASCA, DECIUS, METELLUS, TREBONIUS, CINNA, ANTONY, LEPIDUS, POPILIUS, PUBLIUS, *and others.*

CAES. The ides of March are come.
SOOTH. Ay, Caesar; but not gone.
ART. Hail, Caesar! read this schedule.[1]
DEC. Trebonius doth desire you to o'er-read,
At your best leisure, this his humble suit.
ART. O Caesar, read mine first; for mine's a suit
That touches Caesar nearer: read it, great Caesar.
CAES. What touches us ourself shall be last served.
ART. Delay not, Caesar; read it instantly.
CAES. What, is the fellow mad?
PUB. Sirrah, give place.
CAS. What, urge you your petitions in the street?
Come to the Capitol.

CAESAR *goes up to the Senate-house, the rest following.*

POP. I wish your enterprise to-day may thrive.
CAS. What enterprise, Popilius?
POP. Fare you well. [*Advances to* CAESAR.]
BRU. What said Popilius Lena?
CAS. He wish'd to-day our enterprise might thrive.
I fear our purpose is discovered.
BRU. Look, how he makes to Caesar: mark him.

1. *schedule*] letter.

CAS. Casca,
Be sudden, for we fear prevention.
Brutus, what shall be done? If this be known,
Cassius or Caesar never shall turn back,
For I will slay myself.

BRU. Cassius, be constant:
Popilius Lena speaks not of our purposes;
For, look, he smiles, and Caesar doth not change.[2]

CAS. Trebonius knows his time; for, look you, Brutus,
He draws Mark Antony out of the way.
[*Exeunt* ANTONY *and* TREBONIUS.]

DEC. Where is Metellus Cimber? Let him go,
And presently prefer his suit to Caesar.

BRU. He is address'd:[3] press near and second him.

CIN. Casca, you are the first that rears your hand.

CAES. Are we all ready? What is now amiss
That Caesar and his senate must redress?

MET. Most high, most mighty and most puissant Caesar,
Metellus Cimber throws before thy seat
An humble heart:— [*Kneeling.*]

CAES. I must prevent[4] thee, Cimber.
These couchings[5] and these lowly courtesies
Might fire the blood of ordinary men,
And turn pre-ordinance and first decree
Into the law of children. Be not fond,[6]
To think that Caesar bears such rebel blood
That will be thaw'd from the true quality
With that which melteth fools, I mean, sweet words,
Low-crooked court'sies and base spaniel-fawning.
Thy brother by decree is banished:
If thou dost bend and pray and fawn for him,
I spurn thee like a cur out of my way.
Know, Caesar doth not wrong, nor without cause
Will he be satisfied.

MET. Is there no voice more worthy than my own,
To sound more sweetly in great Caesar's ear

2. *change*] change color, turn pale.
3. *address'd*] ready.
4. *prevent*] anticipate.
5. *couchings*] stoopings.
6. *fond*] foolish.

For the repealing of my banish'd brother?
BRU. I kiss thy hand, but not in flattery, Caesar,
Desiring thee that Publius Cimber may
Have an immediate freedom of repeal.
CAES. What, Brutus!
CAS. Pardon, Caesar; Caesar, pardon:
As low as to thy foot doth Cassius fall,
To beg enfranchisement for Publius Cimber.
CAES. I could be well moved, if I were as you;
If I could pray to move, prayers would move me:
But I am constant as the northern star,
Of whose true-fix'd and resting[7] quality
There is no fellow in the firmament.
The skies are painted with unnumber'd sparks;
They are all fire and every one doth shine;
But there's but one in all doth hold his place:
So in the world; 't is furnish'd well with men,
And men are flesh and blood, and apprehensive:[8]
Yet in the number I do know but one
That unassailable holds on his rank,[9]
Unshaked of motion: and that I am he,
Let me a little show it, even in this;
That I was constant Cimber should be banish'd,
And constant do remain to keep him so.
CIN. O Caesar,—
CAES. Hence! wilt thou lift up Olympus?
DEC. Great Caesar,—
CAES. Doth not Brutus bootless[10] kneel?
CASCA. Speak, hands, for me!
[CASCA *first, then the other* Conspirators *and* MARCUS BRUTUS *stab* CAESAR.]
CAES. Et tu, Brute? Then fall, Caesar! [*Dies.*]
CIN. Liberty! freedom! Tyranny is dead!
Run hence, proclaim, cry it about the streets.
CAS. Some to the common pulpits,[11] and cry out
"Liberty, freedom and enfranchisement!"
BRU. People, and senators, be not affrighted;

7. *resting*] immovable.
8. *apprehensive*] endowed with intelligence.
9. *rank*] position.
10. *bootless*] in vain.
11. *common pulpits*] public rostra.

Fly not; stand still: ambition's debt is paid.
CASCA. Go to the pulpit, Brutus.
DEC. And Cassius too.
BRU. Where's Publius?
CIN. Here, quite confounded with this mutiny.
MET. Stand fast together, lest some friend of Caesar's
Should chance—
BRU. Talk not of standing. Publius, good cheer;
There is no harm intended to your person,
Nor to no Roman else: so tell them, Publius.
CAS. And leave us, Publius; lest that the people
Rushing on us should do your age some mischief.
BRU. Do so: and let no man abide[12] this deed
But we the doers.

Re-enter TREBONIUS.

CAS. Where is Antony?
TRE. Fled to his house amazed:
Men, wives and children stare, cry out and run
As it were doomsday.
BRU. Fates, we will know your pleasures:
That we shall die, we know; 't is but the time,
And drawing days out, that men stand upon.[13]
CAS. Why, he that cuts off twenty years of life
Cuts off so many years of fearing death.
BRU. Grant that, and then is death a benefit:
So are we Caesar's friends, that have abridged
His time of fearing death. Stoop, Romans, stoop,
And let us bathe our hands in Caesar's blood
Up to the elbows, and besmear our swords:
Then walk we forth, even to the market-place,
And waving our red weapons o'er our heads,
Let's all cry "Peace, freedom and liberty!"
CAS. Stoop then, and wash. How many ages hence
Shall this our lofty scene be acted over
In states unborn and accents yet unknown!
BRU. How many times shall Caesar bleed in sport,
That now on Pompey's basis[14] lies along
No worthier than the dust!

12. *abide*] suffer the consequences of.
13. *stand upon*] make of importance.
14. *Pompey's basis*] the base of Pompey's statue.

CAS. So oft as that shall be,
So often shall the knot[15] of us be call'd
The men that gave their country liberty.
DEC. What, shall we forth?
CAS. Ay, every man away:
Brutus shall lead, and we will grace his heels
With the most boldest and best hearts of Rome.

Enter a Servant.

BRU. Soft! who comes here? A friend of Antony's.
SERV. Thus, Brutus, did my master bid me kneel;
Thus did Mark Antony bid me fall down;
And, being prostrate, thus he bade me say:
Brutus is noble, wise, valiant and honest;
Caesar was mighty, bold, royal and loving:
Say I love Brutus and I honour him;
Say I fear'd Caesar, honour'd him and loved him.
If Brutus will vouchsafe that Antony
May safely come to him and be resolved[16]
How Caesar hath deserved to lie in death,
Mark Antony shall not love Caesar dead
So well as Brutus living, but will follow
The fortunes and affairs of noble Brutus
Thorough[17] the hazards of this untrod state
With all true faith. So says my master Antony.
BRU. Thy master is a wise and valiant Roman;
I never thought him worse.
Tell him, so please him come unto this place,
He shall be satisfied and, by my honour,
Depart untouch'd.
SERV. I'll fetch him presently. [*Exit.*]
BRU. I know that we shall have him well to friend.[18]
CAS. I wish we may: but yet have I a mind
That fears him much, and my misgiving still
Falls shrewdly to the purpose.

Re-enter ANTONY.

BRU. But here comes Antony. Welcome, Mark Antony.

15. *knot*] band.
16. *resolved*] informed.
17. *Thorough*] through.
18. *to friend*] for a friend.

ANT. O mighty Caesar! dost thou lie so low?
Are all thy conquests, glories, triumphs, spoils,
Shrunk to this little measure? Fare thee well.
I know not, gentlemen, what you intend,
Who else must be let blood, who else is rank:[19]
If I myself, there is no hour so fit
As Caesar's death's hour, nor no instrument
Of half that worth as those your swords, made rich
With the most noble blood of all this world.
I do beseech ye, if you bear me hard,[20]
Now, whilst your purpled hands do reek and smoke,
Fulfil your pleasure. Live[21] a thousand years,
I shall not find myself so apt to die:
No place will please me so, no mean of death,
As here by Caesar, and by you cut off,
The choice and master spirits of this age.

BRU. O Antony, beg not your death of us.
Though now we must appear bloody and cruel,
As, by our hands and this our present act,
You see we do; yet see you but our hands
And this the bleeding business they have done:
Our hearts you see not; they are pitiful;
And pity to the general wrong of Rome—
As fire drives out fire, so pity pity—
Hath done this deed on Caesar. For your part,
To you our swords have leaden points, Mark Antony:
Our arms in strength of malice, and our hearts
Of brothers' temper, do receive you in
With all kind love, good thoughts and reverence.

CAS. Your voice shall be as strong as any man's
In the disposing of new dignities.[22]

BRU. Only be patient till we have appeased
The multitude, beside themselves with fear,
And then we will deliver you the cause
Why I, that did love Caesar when I struck him,
Have thus proceeded.

ANT. I doubt not of your wisdom.

19. *rank*] diseased (hypertrophic).
20. *bear me hard*] harbor a grudge against me.
21. *Live*] should I live.
22. *dignities*] high offices of state.

Let each man render me his bloody hand:
First, Marcus Brutus, will I shake with you;
Next, Caius Cassius, do I take your hand;
Now, Decius Brutus, yours; now yours, Metellus;
Yours, Cinna; and, my valiant Casca, yours;
Though last, not least in love, yours, good Trebonius.
Gentlemen all,—alas, what shall I say?
My credit now stands on such slippery ground,
That one of two bad ways you must conceit me,[23]
Either a coward or a flatterer.
That I did love thee, Caesar, O, 't is true:
If then thy spirit look upon us now,
Shall it not grieve thee dearer than thy death,
To see thy Antony making his peace,
Shaking the bloody fingers of thy foes,
Most noble! in the presence of thy corse?
Had I as many eyes as thou hast wounds,
Weeping as fast as they stream forth thy blood,
It would become me better than to close
In terms of friendship with thine enemies.
Pardon me, Julius! Here wast thou bay'd, brave hart;[24]
Here didst thou fall, and here thy hunters stand,
Sign'd in thy spoil[25] and crimson'd in thy lethe.[26]
O world, thou wast the forest to this hart;
And this, indeed, O world, the heart of thee.
How like a deer strucken by many princes
Dost thou here lie!

CAS. Mark Antony,—

ANT. Pardon me, Caius Cassius:
The enemies of Caesar shall say this;
Then, in a friend, it is cold modesty.[27]

CAS. I blame you not for praising Caesar so;
But what compact mean you to have with us?
Will you be prick'd in number of[28] our friends,
Or shall we on, and not depend on you?

ANT. Therefore I took your hands, but was indeed

23. *conceit me*] think of me.
24. *bay'd, brave hart*] brought to bay, like a deer hunted by hounds.
25. *spoil*] slaughter.
26. *lethe*] death, oblivion.
27. *modesty*] moderation.
28. *prick'd in number of*] enrolled amongst.

Sway'd from the point by looking down on Caesar.
Friends am I with you all and love you all,
Upon this hope that you shall give me reasons
Why and wherein Caesar was dangerous.

BRU. Or else were this a savage spectacle:
Our reasons are so full of good regard[29]
That were you, Antony, the son of Caesar,
You should be satisfied.

ANT. That's all I seek:
And am moreover suitor that I may
Produce his body to the market-place,[30]
And in the pulpit, as becomes a friend,
Speak in the order of his funeral.

BRU. You shall, Mark Antony.

CAS. Brutus, a word with you.
[*Aside to* BRU.] You know not what you do: do not consent
That Antony speak in his funeral:
Know you how much the people may be moved
By that which he will utter?

BRU. By your pardon:
I will myself into the pulpit first,
And show the reason of our Caesar's death:
What Antony shall speak, I will protest
He speaks by leave and by permission,
And that we are contented Caesar shall
Have all true rites and lawful ceremonies.
It shall advantage more than do us wrong.

CAS. I know not what may fall; I like it not.

BRU. Mark Antony, here, take you Caesar's body.
You shall not in your funeral speech blame us,
But speak all good you can devise of Caesar,
And say you do't by our permission;
Else shall you not have any hand at all
About his funeral: and you shall speak
In the same pulpit whereto I am going,
After my speech is ended.

ANT. Be it so;
I do desire no more.

29. *good regard*] just consideration.
30. *Produce . . . market-place*] carry his body to the Forum.

BRU. Prepare the body then, and follow us. [*Exeunt all but* ANTONY.]
ANT. O, pardon me, thou bleeding piece of earth,
That I am meek and gentle with these butchers!
Thou art the ruins of the noblest man
That ever lived in the tide of times.
Woe to the hand that shed this costly blood!
Over thy wounds now do I prophesy,
Which like dumb mouths do ope their ruby lips
To beg the voice and utterance of my tongue,
A curse shall light upon the limbs of men;
Domestic fury and fierce civil strife
Shall cumber all the parts of Italy;
Blood and destruction shall be so in use,
And dreadful objects so familiar,
That mothers shall but smile when they behold
Their infants quarter'd[31] with the hands of war;
All pity choked with custom of fell deeds:
And Caesar's spirit ranging for revenge,
With Ate[32] by his side come hot from hell,
Shall in these confines with a monarch's voice
Cry "Havoc,"[33] and let slip the dogs of war;
That this foul deed shall smell above the earth
With carrion men, groaning for burial.

Enter a Servant.

You serve Octavius Caesar, do you not?
SERV. I do, Mark Antony.
ANT. Caesar did write for him to come to Rome.
SERV. He did receive his letters, and is coming;
And bid me say to you by word of mouth—
O Caesar! [*Seeing the body.*]
ANT. Thy heart is big; get thee apart and weep.
Passion, I see, is catching, for mine eyes,
Seeing those beads of sorrow stand in thine,
Began to water. Is thy master coming?
SERV. He lies to-night within seven leagues of Rome.
ANT. Post back with speed, and tell him what hath chanced:
Here is a mourning Rome, a dangerous Rome,

31. *quarter'd*] cut to pieces.
32. *Ate*] the goddess of discord in Greek mythology.
33. *"Havoc"*] the signal for pillage and slaughter.

No Rome of safety for Octavius yet;
Hie hence, and tell him so. Yet stay awhile;
Thou shalt not back till I have borne this corse
Into the market-place: there shall I try,
In my oration, how the people take
The cruel issue[34] of these bloody men;
According to the which, thou shalt discourse
To young Octavius of the state of things.
Lend me your hand. [*Exeunt with* CAESAR'S *body.*]

Scene II—The Forum

Enter BRUTUS *and* CASSIUS, *and a throng of* Citizens.

CITIZENS. We will be satisfied; let us be satisfied.
BRU. Then follow me, and give me audience, friends.
Cassius, go you into the other street,
And part the numbers.[1]
Those that will hear me speak, let 'em stay here;
Those that will follow Cassius, go with him;
And public reasons shall be rendered
Of Caesar's death.
FIRST CIT. I will hear Brutus speak.
SEC. CIT. I will hear Cassius; and compare their reasons,
When severally we hear them rendered.
[*Exit* CASSIUS, *with some of the* Citizens.
BRUTUS *goes into the pulpit.*]
THIRD CIT. The noble Brutus is ascended: silence!
BRU. Be patient till the last.
Romans, countrymen, and lovers![2] hear me for my cause, and be silent, that you may hear: believe me for mine honour, and have respect to mine honour, that you may believe: censure[3] me in your wisdom, and awake your senses, that you may the

34. *issue*] action.

1. *part the numbers*] divide up the crowd.
2. *lovers*] friends.
3. *censure*] judge.

better judge. If there be any in this assembly, any dear friend of Caesar's, to him I say that Brutus' love to Caesar was no less than his. If then that friend demand why Brutus rose against Caesar, this is my answer: not that I loved Caesar less, but that I loved Rome more. Had you rather Caesar were living, and die all slaves, than that Caesar were dead, to live all freemen? As Caesar loved me, I weep for him; as he was fortunate, I rejoice at it; as he was valiant, I honour him; but as he was ambitious, I slew him. There is tears for his love; joy for his fortune; honour for his valour; and death for his ambition. Who is here so base that would be a bondman? If any, speak; for him have I offended. Who is here so rude[4] that would not be a Roman? If any, speak; for him have I offended. Who is here so vile that will not love his country? If any, speak; for him have I offended. I pause for a reply.

ALL. None, Brutus, none.

BRU. Then none have I offended. I have done no more to Caesar than you shall do to Brutus. The question of his death is enrolled in the Capitol;[5] his glory not extenuated,[6] wherein he was worthy, nor his offences enforced,[7] for which he suffered death.

Enter ANTONY *and others, with* CAESAR'S *body.*

Here comes his body, mourned by Mark Antony: who, though he had no hand in his death, shall receive the benefit of his dying, a place in the commonwealth; as which of you shall not? With this I depart,—that, as I slew my best lover[8] for the good of Rome, I have the same dagger for myself, when it shall please my country to need my death.

ALL. Live, Brutus! live, live!

FIRST CIT. Bring him with triumph home unto his house.

SEC. CIT. Give him a statue with his ancestors.

THIRD CIT. Let him be Caesar.

FOURTH CIT. Caesar's better parts
Shall be crown'd in Brutus.

FIRST CIT. We'll bring him to his house with shouts and clamours.

BRU. My countrymen,—

4. *rude*] uncivilized.
5. *The question . . . Capitol*] the reasons for his death are recorded in the records of the Senate.
6. *extenuated*] diminished.
7. *enforced*] exaggerated.
8. *lover*] friend.

SEC. CIT. Peace! silence! Brutus speaks.
FIRST CIT. Peace, ho!
BRU. Good countrymen, let me depart alone,
And, for my sake, stay here with Antony:
Do grace to Caesar's corpse, and grace his speech
Tending to Caesar's glories, which Mark Antony
By our permission is allow'd to make.
I do entreat you, not a man depart,
Save I alone, till Antony have spoke. [*Exit.*]
FIRST CIT. Stay, ho! and let us hear Mark Antony.
THIRD CIT. Let him go up into the public chair;[9]
We'll hear him. Noble Antony, go up.
ANT. For Brutus' sake, I am beholding[10] to you. [*Goes into the pulpit.*]
FOURTH CIT. What does he say of Brutus?
THIRD CIT. He says, for Brutus' sake,
He finds himself beholding to us all.
FOURTH CIT. 'T were best he speak no harm of Brutus here.
FIRST CIT. This Caesar was a tyrant.
THIRD CIT. Nay, that's certain:
We are blest that Rome is rid of him.
SEC. CIT. Peace! let us hear what Antony can say.
ANT. You gentle Romans,—
ALL. Peace, ho! Let us hear him.
ANT. Friends, Romans, countrymen, lend me your ears;
I come to bury Caesar, not to praise him.
The evil that men do lives after them;
The good is oft interred with their bones;
So let it be with Caesar. The noble Brutus
Hath told you Caesar was ambitious:
If it were so, it was a grievous fault,
And grievously hath Caesar answer'd it.[11]
Here, under leave of Brutus and the rest,—
For Brutus is an honourable man;
So are they all, all honourable men,—
Come I to speak in Caesar's funeral.
He was my friend, faithful and just to me:
But Brutus says he was ambitious;

9. *the public chair*] the public rostrum (in the Forum).
10. *beholding*] under obligation.
11. *answer'd it*] atoned for it.

And Brutus is an honourable man.
He hath brought many captives home to Rome,
Whose ransoms did the general coffers fill:
Did this in Caesar seem ambitious?
When that the poor have cried, Caesar hath wept:
Ambition should be made of sterner stuff:
Yet Brutus says he was ambitious;
And Brutus is an honourable man.
You all did see that on the Lupercal
I thrice presented him a kingly crown,
Which he did thrice refuse: was this ambition?
Yet Brutus says he was ambitious;
And, sure, he is an honourable man.
I speak not to disprove what Brutus spoke,
But here I am to speak what I do know.
You all did love him once, not without cause:
What cause withholds you then to mourn for him?
O judgement! thou art fled to brutish beasts,
And men have lost their reason. Bear with me;
My heart is in the coffin there with Caesar,
And I must pause till it come back to me.

FIRST CIT. Methinks there is much reason in his sayings.

SEC. CIT. If thou consider rightly of the matter,
Caesar has had great wrong.

THIRD CIT. Has he, masters?
I fear there will a worse come in his place.

FOURTH CIT. Mark'd ye his words? He would not take the crown;
Therefore 't is certain he was not ambitious.

FIRST CIT. If it be found so, some will dear abide[12] it.

SEC. CIT. Poor soul! his eyes are red as fire with weeping.

THIRD CIT. There's not a nobler man in Rome than Antony.

FOURTH CIT. Now mark him, he begins again to speak.

ANT. But yesterday the word of Caesar might
Have stood against the world: now lies he there,
And none so poor to do him reverence.
O masters, if I were disposed to stir
Your hearts and minds to mutiny and rage,
I should do Brutus wrong and Cassius wrong,
Who, you all know, are honourable men:
I will not do them wrong; I rather choose

12. *dear abide*] suffer bitterly for.

To wrong the dead, to wrong myself and you,
Than I will wrong such honourable men.
But here's a parchment with the seal of Caesar;
I found it in his closet; 't is his will:
Let but the commons hear this testament—
Which, pardon me, I do not mean to read—
And they would go and kiss dead Caesar's wounds
And dip their napkins[13] in his sacred blood,
Yea, beg a hair of him for memory,
And, dying, mention it within their wills,
Bequeathing it as a rich legacy
Unto their issue.

FOURTH CIT. We'll hear the will: read it, Mark Antony.

ALL. The will, the will! we will hear Caesar's will.

ANT. Have patience, gentle friends, I must not read it;
It is not meet you know how Caesar loved you.
You are not wood, you are not stones, but men;
And, being men, hearing the will of Caesar,
It will inflame you, it will make you mad:
'T is good you know not that you are his heirs;
For if you should, O, what would come of it!

FOURTH CIT. Read the will; we'll hear it, Antony;
You shall read us the will, Caesar's will.

ANT. Will you be patient? will you stay a while?
I have o'ershot myself[14] to tell you of it:
I fear I wrong the honourable men
Whose daggers have stabb'd Caesar; I do fear it.

FOURTH CIT. They were traitors: honourable men!

ALL. The will! the testament!

SEC. CIT. They were villains, murderers: the will! read the will.

ANT. You will compel me then to read the will?
Then make a ring about the corpse of Caesar,
And let me show you him that made the will.
Shall I descend? and will you give me leave?

ALL. Come down.

SEC. CIT. Descend. [*He comes down from the pulpit.*]

THIRD CIT. You shall have leave.

FOURTH CIT. A ring; stand round.

FIRST CIT. Stand from the hearse, stand from the body.

13. *napkins*] handkerchiefs.
14. *o'ershot myself*] gone beyond my intention.

SEC. CIT. Room for Antony, most noble Antony.
ANT. Nay, press not so upon me; stand far off.
ALL. Stand back. Room! Bear back.
ANT. If you have tears, prepare to shed them now.
You all do know this mantle: I remember
The first time ever Caesar put it on;
'T was on a summer's evening, in his tent,
That day he overcame the Nervii:[15]
Look, in this place ran Cassius' dagger through:
See what a rent the envious[16] Casca made:
Through this the well-beloved Brutus stabb'd;
And as he pluck'd his cursed steel away,
Mark how the blood of Caesar follow'd it,
As rushing out of doors, to be resolved[17]
If Brutus so unkindly knock'd, or no:
For Brutus, as you know, was Caesar's angel:[18]
Judge, O you gods, how dearly Caesar loved him!
This was the most unkindest cut of all;
For when the noble Caesar saw him stab,
Ingratitude, more strong than traitors' arms,
Quite vanquish'd him: then burst his mighty heart;
And, in his mantle muffling up his face,
Even at the base of Pompey's statue,
Which all the while ran blood, great Caesar fell.
O, what a fall was there, my countrymen!
Then I, and you, and all of us fell down,
Whilst bloody treason flourish'd over us.
O, now you weep, and I perceive you feel
The dint[19] of pity: these are gracious drops.
Kind souls, what weep you when you but behold
Our Caesar's vesture wounded? Look you here,
Here is himself, marr'd, as you see, with[20] traitors.
FIRST CIT. O piteous spectacle!
SEC. CIT. O noble Caesar!
THIRD CIT. O woful day!
FOURTH CIT. O traitors, villains!

15. *Nervii*] a warlike Belgian tribe.
16. *envious*] malicious.
17. *to be resolved*] to ascertain.
18. *angel*] dearest friend.
19. *dint*] stroke or impression.
20. *marr'd . . . with*] defaced by.

FIRST CIT. O most bloody sight!
SEC. CIT. We will be revenged.
ALL. Revenge! About! Seek! Burn! Fire! Kill! Slay! Let not a traitor live!
ANT. Stay, countrymen.
FIRST CIT. Peace there! hear the noble Antony.
SEC. CIT. We'll hear him, we'll follow him, we'll die with him.
ANT. Good friends, sweet friends, let me not stir you up
To such a sudden flood of mutiny.
They that have done this deed are honourable;
What private griefs[21] they have, alas, I know not,
That made them do it: they are wise and honourable,
And will, no doubt, with reasons answer you.
I come not, friends, to steal away your hearts:
I am no orator, as Brutus is;
But, as you know me all, a plain blunt man,
That love my friend; and that they know full well
That gave me public leave to speak of him:
For I have neither wit,[22] nor words, nor worth,
Action,[23] nor utterance, nor the power of speech,
To stir men's blood: I only speak right on;
I tell you that which you yourselves do know;
Show you sweet Caesar's wounds, poor poor dumb mouths,
And bid them speak for me: but were I Brutus,
And Brutus Antony, there were an Antony
Would ruffle up your spirits, and put a tongue
In every wound of Caesar, that should move
The stones of Rome to rise and mutiny.
ALL. We'll mutiny.
FIRST CIT. We'll burn the house of Brutus.
THIRD CIT. Away, then! come, seek the conspirators.
ANT. Yet hear me, countrymen; yet hear me speak.
ALL. Peace, ho! Hear Antony. Most noble Antony!
ANT. Why, friends, you go to do you know not what:
Wherein hath Caesar thus deserved your loves?
Alas, you know not; I must tell you then:
You have forgot the will I told you of.
ALL. Most true: the will! Let's stay and hear the will.
ANT. Here is the will, and under Caesar's seal.

21. *private griefs*] personal grievances.
22. *wit*] intelligence, imagination.
23. *Action*] gesture.

To every Roman citizen he gives,
To every several[24] man, seventy-five drachmas.[25]
SEC. CIT. Most noble Caesar! we'll revenge his death.
THIRD CIT. O royal Caesar!
ANT. Hear me with patience.
ALL. Peace, ho!
ANT. Moreover, he hath left you all his walks,[26]
His private arbours and new-planted orchards,
On this side Tiber; he hath left them you,
And to your heirs for ever; common pleasures,[27]
To walk abroad and recreate yourselves.
Here was a Caesar! when comes such another?
FIRST CIT. Never, never. Come, away, away!
We'll burn his body in the holy place,
And with the brands fire the traitors' houses.
Take up the body.
SEC. CIT. Go fetch fire.
THIRD CIT. Pluck down benches.
FOURTH CIT. Pluck down forms,[28] windows, any thing.
[*Exeunt* Citizens *with the body.*]
ANT. Now let it work. Mischief, thou art afoot,
Take thou what course thou wilt.

Enter a Servant.

How now, fellow!
SERV. Sir, Octavius is already come to Rome.
ANT. Where is he?
SERV. He and Lepidus are at Caesar's house.
ANT. And thither will I straight to visit him:
He comes upon a wish. Fortune is merry,
And in this mood will give us any thing.
SERV. I heard him say, Brutus and Cassius
Are rid[29] like madmen through the gates of Rome.
ANT. Belike they had some notice of the people,
How I had moved them. Bring me to Octavius. [*Exeunt.*]

24. *several*] single, individual.
25. *drachmas*] ancient Greek silver coins.
26. *walks*] parks, gardens.
27. *common pleasures*] public pleasure grounds.
28. *forms*] benches.
29. *Are rid*] have ridden.

Scene III—A street

Enter CINNA *the poet.*

CIN. I dreamt to-night that I did feast with Caesar,
And things unluckily charge my fantasy:[1]
I have no will to wander forth of doors,
Yet something leads me forth.

Enter Citizens.

FIRST CIT. What is your name?
SEC. CIT. Whither are you going?
THIRD CIT. Where do you dwell?
FOURTH CIT. Are you a married man or a bachelor?
SEC. CIT. Answer every man directly.
FIRST CIT. Ay, and briefly.
FOURTH CIT. Ay, and wisely.
THIRD CIT. Ay, and truly, you were best.[2]
CIN. What is my name? Whither am I going? Where do I dwell? Am I a married man or a bachelor? Then, to answer every man directly and briefly, wisely and truly: wisely I say, I am a bachelor.
SEC. CIT. That's as much as to say, they are fools that marry: you'll bear me a bang[3] for that, I fear. Proceed; directly.
CIN. Directly, I am going to Caesar's funeral.
FIRST CIT. As a friend or an enemy?
CIN. As a friend.
SEC. CIT. That matter is answered directly.
FOURTH CIT. For your dwelling, briefly.
CIN. Briefly, I dwell by the Capitol.
THIRD CIT. Your name, sir, truly.
CIN. Truly, my name is Cinna.
FIRST CIT. Tear him to pieces; he's a conspirator.
CIN. I am Cinna the poet, I am Cinna the poet.
FOURTH CIT. Tear him for his bad verses, tear him for his bad verses.
CIN. I am not Cinna the conspirator.
FOURTH CIT. It is no matter, his name's Cinna; pluck but his name out of his heart, and turn him going.
THIRD CIT. Tear him, tear him! Come, brands, ho! fire-brands: to Brutus', to Cassius'; burn all: some to Decius' house, and some to Casca's; some to Ligarius': away, go! [*Exeunt.*]

1. *unluckily . . . fantasy*] ominously oppress my imagination.
2. *you were best*] it would be best for you.
3. *bear me a bang*] receive a blow from me.

Act IV—Scene I

A HOUSE IN ROME

ANTONY, OCTAVIUS, *and* LEPIDUS, *seated at a table.*

ANT. These many then shall die; their names are prick'd.[1]
OCT. Your brother too must die; consent you, Lepidus?
LEP. I do consent—
OCT. Prick him down, Antony.
LEP. Upon condition Publius shall not live,
Who is your sister's son, Mark Antony.
ANT. He shall not live; look, with a spot[2] I damn him.
But, Lepidus, go you to Caesar's house;
Fetch the will hither, and we shall determine
How to cut off some charge in legacies.
LEP. What, shall I find you here?
OCT. Or here, or at the Capitol. [*Exit* LEPIDUS.]
ANT. This is a slight unmeritable[3] man,
Meet to be sent on errands: is it fit,
The three-fold world[4] divided, he should stand
One of the three to share it?
OCT. So you thought him,
And took his voice who should be prick'd to die
In our black sentence and proscription.
ANT. Octavius, I have seen more days than you:
And though we lay these honours on this man,
To ease ourselves of divers slanderous loads,
He shall but bear them as the ass bears gold,

1. *prick'd*] put on the list.
2. *spot*] mark (made by a stylus).
3. *slight unmeritable*] insignificant, undeserving.
4. *The three-fold world*] Europe, Asia and Africa.

To groan and sweat under the business,
Either led or driven, as we point the way;
And having brought our treasure where we will,
Then take we down his load and turn him off,
Like to the empty ass, to shake his ears
And graze in commons.[5]

OCT. You may do your will:
But he's a tried and valiant soldier.

ANT. So is my horse, Octavius, and for that
I do appoint him store of provender:
It is a creature that I teach to fight,
To wind,[6] to stop, to run directly on,
His corporal motion govern'd by my spirit.
And, in some taste,[7] is Lepidus but so;
He must be taught, and train'd, and bid go forth;
A barren-spirited fellow; one that feeds
On abjects, orts[8] and imitations,
Which, out of use and staled[9] by other men,
Begin his fashion:[10] do not talk of him
But as a property.[11] And now, Octavius,
Listen great things: Brutus and Cassius
Are levying powers: we must straight make head:[12]
Therefore let our alliance be combined,
Our best friends made, our means stretch'd;
And let us presently go sit in council,
How covert matters may be best disclosed,
And open perils surest answered.

OCT. Let us do so: for we are at the stake,[13]
And bay'd about[14] with many enemies;
And some that smile have in their hearts, I fear,
Millions of mischiefs. [*Exeunt.*]

5. *commons*] public pasture.
6. *wind*] turn.
7. *in some taste*] in some slight degree.
8. *abjects, orts*] forsaken persons and refuse.
9. *staled*] worn-out, rendered obsolete.
10. *Begin his fashion*] form the starting point of his own fashion.
11. *a property*] a theatrical property, a mere tool.
12. *make head*] raise an army.
13. *at the stake*] like a bear tied to a stake in the sport of bearbaiting.
14. *bay'd about*] barked at.

Scene II—Camp near Sardis

BEFORE BRUTUS'S TENT

Drum. Enter BRUTUS, LUCILIUS, LUCIUS, *and* Soldiers; TITINIUS *and* PINDARUS *meet them.*

BRU. Stand, ho!
LUCIL. Give the word, ho! and stand.
BRU. What now, Lucilius! is Cassius near?
LUCIL. He is at hand; and Pindarus is come
To do you salutation from his master.
BRU. He greets me well. Your master, Pindarus,
In his own change,[1] or by ill officers,
Hath given me some worthy cause to wish
Things done undone: but if he be at hand,
I shall be satisfied.
PIN. I do not doubt
But that my noble master will appear
Such as he is, full of regard and honour.
BRU. He is not doubted. A word, Lucilius,
How he received you: let me be resolved.
LUCIL. With courtesy and with respect enough;
But not with such familiar instances,[2]
Nor with such free and friendly conference,
As he hath used of old.
BRU. Thou hast described
A hot friend cooling: ever note, Lucilius,
When love begins to sicken and decay,
It useth an enforced ceremony.
There are no tricks in plain and simple faith:
But hollow[3] men, like horses hot at hand,[4]
Make gallant show and promise of their mettle;
But when they should endure the bloody spur,
They fall their crests[5] and like deceitful jades[6]
Sink in the trial. Comes his army on?

1. *In his own change*] because of some change of mind on his own part.
2. *familiar instances*] marks of familiarity.
3. *hollow*] insincere.
4. *hot at hand*] spirited when reined in.
5. *fall their crests*] lower their heads.
6. *deceitful jades*] horses not to be trusted.

LUCIL. They mean this night in Sardis to be quarter'd;
The greater part, the horse in general,
Are come with Cassius. [*Low march within.*]
BRU. Hark! he is arrived:
March gently on to meet him.

Enter CASSIUS *and his powers.*

CAS. Stand, ho!
BRU. Stand, ho! Speak the word along.
FIRST SOL. Stand!
SEC. SOL. Stand!
THIRD SOL. Stand!
CAS. Most noble brother, you have done me wrong.
BRU. Judge me, you gods! wrong I mine enemies?
And, if not so, how should I wrong a brother?
CAS. Brutus, this sober form of yours hides wrongs;
And when you do them—
BRU. Cassius, be content;
Speak your griefs[7] softly: I do know you well.
Before the eyes of both our armies here,
Which should perceive nothing but love from us,
Let us not wrangle: bid them move away;
Then in my tent, Cassius, enlarge your griefs,[8]
And I will give you audience.
CAS. Pindarus,
Bid our commanders lead their charges[9] off
A little from this ground.
BRU. Lucilius, do you the like, and let no man
Come to our tent till we have done our conference.
Let Lucius and Titinius guard our door. [*Exeunt.*]

7. *griefs*] grievances.
8. *enlarge your griefs*] set out in full your grievances.
9. *charges*] troops.

Scene III—Brutus's tent

Enter BRUTUS *and* CASSIUS.

CAS. That you have wrong'd me doth appear in this:
You have condemn'd and noted[1] Lucius Pella
For taking bribes here of the Sardians;
Wherein my letters, praying on his side,
Because I knew the man, were slighted off.[2]
BRU. You wrong'd yourself to write in such a case.
CAS. In such a time as this it is not meet
That every nice[3] offence should bear his comment.[4]
BRU. Let me tell you, Cassius, you yourself
Are much condemn'd to have an itching palm,
To sell and mart[5] your offices for gold
To undeservers.
CAS. I an itching palm!
You know that you are Brutus that speaks this,
Or, by the gods, this speech were else your last.
BRU. The name of Cassius honours this corruption,
And chastisement doth therefore hide his head.
CAS. Chastisement!
BRU. Remember March, the ides of March remember:
Did not great Julius bleed for justice' sake?
What villain touch'd his body, that did stab,
And not for justice? What, shall one of us,
That struck the foremost man of all this world
But for supporting robbers, shall we now
Contaminate our fingers with base bribes,
And sell the mighty space of our large honours
For so much trash as may be grasped thus?
I had rather be a dog, and bay[6] the moon,
Than such a Roman.
CAS. Brutus, bait not me;

1. *noted*] disgraced.
2. *slighted off*] disregarded.
3. *nice*] petty.
4. *bear his comment*] be scrutinized.
5. *mart*] trade.
6. *bay*] bark at.

I'll not endure it: you forget yourself,
To hedge me in;[7] I am a soldier, I,
Older in practice, abler than yourself
To make conditions.[8]

BRU. Go to; you are not, Cassius.
CAS. I am.
BRU. I say you are not.
CAS. Urge[9] me no more, I shall forget myself;
Have mind upon your health, tempt me no farther.
BRU. Away, slight[10] man!
CAS. Is 't possible?
BRU. Hear me, for I will speak.
Must I give way and room to your rash choler?
Shall I be frighted when a madman stares?
CAS. O ye gods, ye gods! must I endure all this?
BRU. All this! ay, more: fret till your proud heart break;
Go show your slaves how choleric you are,
And make your bondmen tremble. Must I budge?
Must I observe[11] you? must I stand and crouch
Under your testy humour? By the gods,
You shall digest the venom of your spleen,
Though it do split you; for, from this day forth,
I'll use you for my mirth, yea, for my laughter,
When you are waspish.
CAS. Is it come to this?
BRU. You say you are a better soldier:
Let it appear so; make your vaunting true,
And it shall please me well: for mine own part,
I shall be glad to learn of noble men.
CAS. You wrong me every way; you wrong me, Brutus;
I said, an elder soldier, not a better:
Did I say, better?
BRU. If you did, I care not.
CAS. When Caesar lived, he durst not thus have moved me.
BRU. Peace, peace! you durst not so have tempted him.

7. *hedge me in*] limit my authority.
8. *make conditions*] decide the terms on which offices are to be conferred.
9. *Urge*] exasperate.
10. *slight*] insignificant.
11. *observe*] defer to.

CAS. I durst not!
BRU. No.
CAS. What, durst not tempt him!
BRU. For your life you durst not.
CAS. Do not presume too much upon my love;
I may do that I shall be sorry for.
BRU. You have done that you should be sorry for.
There is no terror, Cassius, in your threats;
For I am arm'd so strong in honesty,
That they pass by me as the idle wind
Which I respect not. I did send to you
For certain sums of gold, which you denied me:
For I can raise no money by vile means:
By heaven, I had rather coin my heart,
And drop my blood for drachmas, than to wring
From the hard hands of peasants their vile trash
By any indirection.[12] I did send
To you for gold to pay my legions,
Which you denied me: was that done like Cassius?
Should I have answer'd Caius Cassius so?
When Marcus Brutus grows so covetous,
To lock such rascal counters[13] from his friends,
Be ready, gods, with all your thunderbolts,
Dash him to pieces!
CAS. I denied you not.
BRU. You did.
CAS. I did not: he was but a fool
That brought my answer back. Brutus hath rived my heart:
A friend should bear his friend's infirmities,
But Brutus makes mine greater than they are.
BRU. I do not, till you practise them on me.
CAS. You love me not.
BRU. I do not like your faults.
CAS. A friendly eye could never see such faults.
BRU. A flatterer's would not, though they do appear
As huge as high Olympus.
CAS. Come, Antony, and young Octavius, come,
Revenge yourselves alone on Cassius,
For Cassius is aweary of the world;

12. *indirection*] dishonesty.
13. *rascal counters*] worthless pieces of money.

Hated by one he loves; braved by his brother;
Check'd like a bondman; all his faults observed,
Set in a note-book, learn'd and conn'd by rote,
To cast into my teeth. O, I could weep
My spirit from mine eyes! There is my dagger,
And here my naked breast; within, a heart
Dearer than Plutus' mine, richer than gold:
If that thou be'st a Roman, take it forth;
I, that denied thee gold, will give my heart:
Strike, as thou didst at Caesar; for I know,
When thou didst hate him worst, thou lovedst him better
Than ever thou lovedst Cassius.

BRU. Sheathe your dagger:
Be angry when you will, it shall have scope;
Do what you will, dishonour shall be humour.[14]
O Cassius, you are yoked with a lamb,
That carries anger as the flint bears fire,
Who, much enforced, shows a hasty spark
And straight is cold again.

CAS. Hath Cassius lived
To be but mirth and laughter to his Brutus,
When grief and blood ill-temper'd vexeth him?

BRU. When I spoke that, I was ill-temper'd too.

CAS. Do you confess so much? Give me your hand.

BRU. And my heart too.

CAS. O Brutus!

BRU. What's the matter?

CAS. Have not you love enough to bear with me,
When that rash humour which my mother gave me
Makes me forgetful?

BRU. Yes, Cassius, and from henceforth,
When you are over-earnest with your Brutus,
He'll think your mother chides, and leave you so.

POET. [*Within.*] Let me go in to see the generals;
There is some grudge between 'em; 't is not meet
They be alone.

LUCIL. [*Within.*] You shall not come to them.

POET. [*Within.*] Nothing but death shall stay me.

Enter Poet, *followed by* LUCILIUS, TITINIUS, *and* LUCIUS.

14. *Do . . . humour*] Whatever dishonorable thing you may do, I will set it down to the whim or caprice of the moment.

CAS. How now! what's the matter?
POET. For shame, you generals! what do you mean?
Love, and be friends, as two such men should be;
For I have seen more years, I'm sure, than ye.
CAS. Ha, ha! how vilely doth this cynic[15] rhyme!
BRU. Get you hence, sirrah; saucy fellow, hence!
CAS. Bear with him, Brutus; 't is his fashion.
BRU. I'll know his humour when he knows his time:
What should the wars do with these jigging[16] fools?
Companion,[17] hence!
CAS. Away, away, be gone! [*Exit* Poet.]
BRU. Lucilius and Titinius, bid the commanders
Prepare to lodge their companies to-night.
CAS. And come yourselves, and bring Messala with you
Immediately to us. [*Exeunt* LUCILIUS *and* TITINIUS.]
BRU. Lucius, a bowl of wine! [*Exit* LUCIUS.]
CAS. I did not think you could have been so angry.
BRU. O Cassius, I am sick of many griefs.
CAS. Of your philosophy you make no use,
If you give place to accidental evils.
BRU. No man bears sorrow better: Portia is dead.
CAS. Ha! Portia!
BRU. She is dead.
CAS. How 'scaped I killing when I cross'd you so?
O insupportable and touching loss!
Upon what sickness?
BRU. Impatient of my absence,
And grief that young Octavius with Mark Antony
Have made themselves so strong: for with her death
That tidings came: with this she fell distract,
And, her attendants absent, swallow'd fire.[18]
CAS. And died so?
BRU. Even so.
CAS. O ye immortal gods!

Re-enter LUCIUS, *with wine and taper.*

BRU. Speak no more of her. Give me a bowl of wine.

15. *cynic*] uncouth man.
16. *jigging*] often used of doggerel rhyming, as well as of dancing.
17. *Companion*] fellow (used contemptuously).
18. *swallow'd fire*] According to Plutarch, Portia put burning coals in her mouth, and then kept her lips closed until she choked.

In this I bury all unkindness, Cassius. [*Drinks.*]
CAS. My heart is thirsty for that noble pledge.
Fill, Lucius, till the wine o'erswell the cup;
I cannot drink too much of Brutus' love. [*Drinks.*]
BRU. Come in, Titinius! [*Exit* LUCIUS.]

Re-enter TITINIUS, *with* MESSALA.

Welcome, good Messala.
Now sit we close about this taper here,
And call in question our necessities.
CAS. Portia, art thou gone?
BRU. No more, I pray you.
Messala, I have here received letters,
That young Octavius and Mark Antony
Come down upon us with a mighty power,
Bending their expedition toward Philippi.
MES. Myself have letters of the selfsame tenour.
BRU. With what addition?
MES. That by proscription and bills of outlawry
Octavius, Antony and Lepidus,
Have put to death an hundred senators.
BRU. Therein our letters do not well agree;
Mine speak of seventy senators that died
By their proscriptions, Cicero being one.
CAS. Cicero one!
MES. Cicero is dead,
And by that order of proscription.
Had you your letters from your wife, my lord?
BRU. No, Messala.
MES. Nor nothing in your letters writ of her?
BRU. Nothing, Messala.
MES. That, methinks, is strange.
BRU. Why ask you? hear you ought of her in yours?
MES. No, my lord.
BRU. Now, as you are a Roman, tell me true.
MES. Then like a Roman bear the truth I tell:
For certain she is dead, and by strange manner.
BRU. Why, farewell, Portia. We must die, Messala:
With meditating that she must die once
I have the patience to endure it now.
MES. Even so great men great losses should endure.

CAS. I have as much of this in art[19] as you,
But yet my nature could not bear it so.
BRU. Well, to our work alive. What do you think
Of marching to Philippi presently?
CAS. I do not think it good.
BRU. Your reason?
CAS. This it is:
'T is better that the enemy seek us:
So shall he waste his means, weary his soldiers,
Doing himself offence;[20] whilst we lying still
Are full of rest, defence and nimbleness.
BRU. Good reasons must of force give place to better.
The people 'twixt Philippi and this ground
Do stand but in a forced affection,
For they have grudged us contribution:
The enemy, marching along by them,
By them shall make a fuller number up,
Come on refresh'd, new-added[21] and encouraged;
From which advantage shall we cut him off
If at Philippi we do face him there,
These people at our back.
CAS. Hear me, good brother.
BRU. Under your pardon. You must note beside
That we have tried the utmost of our friends,
Our legions are brim-full, our cause is ripe:
The enemy increaseth every day;
We, at the height, are ready to decline.
There is a tide in the affairs of men
Which taken at the flood leads on to fortune;
Omitted,[22] all the voyage of their life
Is bound in shallows and in miseries.
On such a full sea are we now afloat,
And we must take the current when it serves,
Or lose our ventures.
CAS. Then, with your will, go on;
We'll along ourselves and meet them at Philippi.
BRU. The deep of night is crept upon our talk,

19. *in art*] in theory.
20. *offence*] harm, injury.
21. *new-added*] reinforced.
22. *Omitted*] neglected.

And nature must obey necessity;
Which we will niggard[23] with a little rest.
There is no more to say?
CAS. No more. Good night:
Early to-morrow will we rise and hence.
BRU. Lucius! [*Re-enter* LUCIUS.] My gown. [*Exit* LUCIUS.]
Farewell, good Messala:
Good night, Titinius: noble, noble Cassius,
Good night, and good repose.
CAS. O my dear brother!
This was an ill beginning of the night:
Never come such division 'tween our souls!
Let it not, Brutus.
BRU. Every thing is well.
CAS. Good night, my lord.
BRU. Good night, good brother.
TIT. MES. Good night, Lord Brutus.
BRU. Farewell, every one.
[*Exeunt all but* BRUTUS.]

Re-enter LUCIUS, *with the gown.*

Give me the gown. Where is thy instrument?
LUC. Here in the tent.
BRU. What, thou speak'st drowsily?
Poor knave,[24] I blame thee not; thou art o'er-watch'd.[25]
Call Claudius and some other of my men;
I'll have them sleep on cushions in my tent.
LUC. Varro and Claudius!

Enter VARRO *and* CLAUDIUS.

VAR. Calls my lord?
BRU. I pray you, sirs, lie in my tent and sleep;
It may be I shall raise you by and by
On business to my brother Cassius.
VAR. So please you, we will stand and watch your pleasure.
BRU. I will not have it so: lie down, good sirs;
It may be I shall otherwise bethink me.
Look, Lucius, here's the book I sought for so;

23. *niggard*] satisfy sparingly.
24. *knave*] lad.
25. *o'er-watch'd*] wearied by lack of sleep.

I put it in the pocket of my gown. [VAR. *and* CLAU. *lie down.*]
LUC. I was sure your lordship did not give it me.
BRU. Bear with me, good boy, I am much forgetful.
Canst thou hold up thy heavy eyes a while,
And touch thy instrument a strain or two?
LUC. Ay, my lord, an 't please you.
BRU. It does, my boy:
I trouble thee too much, but thou art willing.
LUC. It is my duty, sir.
BRU. I should not urge thy duty past thy might;
I know young bloods look for a time of rest.
LUC. I have slept, my lord, already.
BRU. It was well done; and thou shalt sleep again;
I will not hold thee long: if I do live,
I will be good to thee. [*Music, and a song.*]
This is a sleepy tune. O murderous slumber,
Lay'st thou thy leaden mace[26] upon my boy,
That plays thee music? Gentle knave, good night;
I will not do thee so much wrong to wake thee:
If thou dost nod, thou break'st thy instrument;
I'll take it from thee; and, good boy, good night.
Let me see, let me see; is not the leaf turn'd down
Where I left reading? Here it is, I think. [*Sits down.*]

Enter the Ghost of CAESAR.

How ill this taper burns! Ha! who comes here?
I think it is the weakness of mine eyes
That shapes this monstrous apparition.
It comes upon me. Art thou any thing?
Art thou some god, some angel, or some devil,
That makest my blood cold, and my hair to stare?[27]
Speak to me what thou art.
GHOST. Thy evil spirit, Brutus.
BRU. Why comest thou?
GHOST. To tell thee thou shalt see me at Philippi.
BRU. Well; then I shall see thee again?
GHOST. Ay, at Philippi.
BRU. Why, I will see thee at Philippi then. [*Exit Ghost.*]
Now I have taken heart thou vanishest.

26. *mace*] scepter.
27. *stare*] stand on end.

Ill spirit, I would hold more talk with thee.
Boy, Lucius! Varro! Claudius! Sirs awake!
Claudius!

LUC. The strings, my lord, are false.

BRU. He thinks he still is at his instrument.
Lucius, awake!

LUC. My lord?

BRU. Didst thou dream, Lucius, that thou so criedst out?

LUC. My lord, I do not know that I did cry.

BRU. Yes, that thou didst: didst thou see any thing?

LUC. Nothing, my lord.

BRU. Sleep again, Lucius. Sirrah Claudius!
[*To* VAR.] Fellow thou, awake!

VAR. My lord?

CLAU. My lord?

BRU. Why did you so cry out, sirs, in your sleep?

VAR. CLAU. Did we, my lord?

BRU. Ay: saw you any thing?

VAR. No, my lord, I saw nothing.

CLAU. Nor I, my lord.

BRU. Go and commend me to my brother Cassius;
Bid him set on his powers betimes before,
And we will follow.

VAR. CLAU. It shall be done, my lord. [*Exeunt.*]

Act V—Scene I

THE PLAINS OF PHILIPPI

Enter OCTAVIUS, ANTONY, *and their* Army.

OCT. Now, Antony, our hopes are answered:
You said the enemy would not come down,
But keep the hills and upper regions;
It proves not so: their battles[1] are at hand;
They mean to warn[2] us at Philippi here,
Answering before we do demand of them.

ANT. Tut, I am in their bosoms, and I know
Wherefore they do it: they could be content
To visit other places; and come down
With fearful bravery,[3] thinking by this face
To fasten in our thoughts that they have courage;
But 't is not so.

Enter a Messenger.

MESS. Prepare you, generals:
The enemy comes on in gallant show;
Their bloody sign of battle is hung out,
And something to be done immediately.

ANT. Octavius, lead your battle softly on,
Upon the left hand of the even field.

OCT. Upon the right hand I; keep thou the left.

ANT. Why do you cross[4] me in this exigent?[5]

1. *battles*] battalions.
2. *warn*] challenge.
3. *fearful bravery*] a timid show of courage.
4. *cross*] contradict.
5. *exigent*] emergency.

OCT. I do not cross you; but I will do so.[6] [*March.*]

Drum. Enter BRUTUS, CASSIUS, *and their* Army; LUCILIUS, TITINIUS, MESSALA, *and others.*

BRU. They stand, and would have parley.
CAS. Stand fast, Titinius: we must out and talk.
OCT. Mark Antony, shall we give sign of battle?
ANT. No, Caesar, we will answer on their charge.[7]
Make forth; the generals would have some words.
OCT. Stir not until the signal.
BRU. Words before blows: is it so, countrymen?
OCT. Not that we love words better, as you do.
BRU. Good words are better than bad strokes, Octavius.
ANT. In your bad strokes, Brutus, you give good words:
Witness the hole you made in Caesar's heart,
Crying "Long live! hail, Caesar!"
CAS. Antony,
The posture[8] of your blows are yet unknown;
But for your words, they rob the Hybla bees,[9]
And leave them honeyless.
ANT. Not stingless too.
BRU. O, yes, and soundless too;
For you have stol'n their buzzing, Antony,
And very wisely threat before you sting.
ANT. Villains, you did not so, when your vile daggers
Hack'd one another in the sides of Caesar:
You show'd your teeth like apes, and fawn'd like hounds,
And bow'd like bondmen, kissing Caesar's feet;
Whilst damned Casca, like a cur, behind
Struck Caesar on the neck. O you flatterers!
CAS. Flatterers! Now, Brutus, thank yourself:
This tongue had not offended so to-day,
If Cassius might have ruled.
OCT. Come, come, the cause: if arguing make us sweat,
The proof of it will turn to redder drops.
Look;

6. *I will do so*] I will have my way.
7. *answer on their charge*] meet them when they charge.
8. *posture*] quality.
9. *the Hybla bees*] Hybla was a town in Sicily celebrated by classical poets for the sweetness of its honey.

I draw a sword against conspirators;
When think you that the sword goes up again?
Never, till Caesar's three and thirty wounds
Be well avenged, or till another Caesar
Have added slaughter to the sword of traitors.

BRU. Caesar, thou canst not die by traitors' hands,
Unless thou bring'st them with thee.

OCT. So I hope;
I was not born to die on Brutus' sword.

BRU. O, if thou wert the noblest of thy strain,
Young man, thou couldst not die more honourable.

CAS. A peevish schoolboy, worthless of such honour,
Join'd with a masker and a reveller!

ANT. Old Cassius still!

OCT. Come, Antony; away!
Defiance, traitors, hurl we in your teeth;
If you dare fight to-day, come to the field:
If not, when you have stomachs.[10]

[*Exeunt* OCTAVIUS, ANTONY, *and their* Army.]

CAS. Why, now, blow wind, swell billow, and swim bark!
The storm is up, and all is on the hazard.

BRU. Ho, Lucilius! hark, a word with you.

LUCIL. [*Standing forth.*] My lord?

[BRUTUS *and* LUCILIUS *converse apart.*]

CAS. Messala!

MES. [*Standing forth.*] What says my general?

CAS. Messala,
This is my birth-day; as[11] this very day
Was Cassius born. Give me thy hand, Messala:
Be thou my witness that, against my will,
As Pompey was, am I compell'd to set
Upon one battle all our liberties.
You know that I held Epicurus[12] strong,
And his opinion: now I change my mind,
And partly credit things that do presage.
Coming from Sardis, on our former[13] ensign
Two mighty eagles fell, and there they perch'd,

10. *stomachs*] inclination.
11. *as*] on.
12. *Epicurus*] the Greek philosopher, who rejected the Stoics' belief in omens.
13. *former*] foremost.

Gorging and feeding from our soldiers' hands;
Who to Philippi here consorted[14] us:
This morning are they fled away and gone;
And in their steads do ravens, crows and kites
Fly o'er our heads and downward look on us,
As we were sickly prey: their shadows seem
A canopy most fatal, under which
Our army lies, ready to give up the ghost.

MES. Believe not so.

CAS. I but believe it partly,
For I am fresh of spirit and resolved
To meet all perils very constantly.

BRU. Even so, Lucilius.

CAS. Now, most noble Brutus,
The gods to-day stand friendly, that we may,
Lovers[15] in peace, lead on our days to age!
But, since the affairs of men rest still incertain,
Let's reason with[16] the worst that may befall.
If we do lose this battle, then is this
The very last time we shall speak together:
What are you then determined to do?

BRU. Even by the rule of that philosophy
By which I did blame Cato[17] for the death
Which he did give himself: I know not how,
But I do find it cowardly and vile,
For fear of what might fall, so to prevent
The time of life:[18] arming myself with patience
To stay[19] the providence of some high powers
That govern us below.

CAS. Then, if we lose this battle,
You are contented to be led in triumph
Thorough the streets of Rome?

BRU. No, Cassius, no: think not, thou noble Roman,
That ever Brutus will go bound to Rome;

14. *consorted*] accompanied.
15. *Lovers*] friends.
16. *reason with*] talk of.
17. *Cato*] the Stoic philosopher, who loyally supported Pompey. After the defeat by Caesar of Pompey's friends at the battle of Thapsus, 46 B.C., Cato committed suicide at Utica, in Africa.
18. *prevent The time of life*] anticipate the normal close of life.
19. *stay*] await.

He bears too great a mind. But this same day
Must end that work the ides of March begun;
And whether we shall meet again I know not.
Therefore our everlasting farewell take.
For ever, and for ever, farewell, Cassius!
If we do meet again, why, we shall smile;
If not, why then this parting was well made.

CAS. For ever and for ever farewell, Brutus!
If we do meet again, we'll smile indeed;
If not, 't is true this parting was well made.

BRU. Why then, lead on. O, that a man might know
The end of this day's business ere it come!
But it sufficeth that the day will end,
And then the end is known. Come, ho! away! [*Exeunt.*]

Scene II—The field of battle

Alarum. Enter BRUTUS *and* MESSALA.

BRU. Ride, ride, Messala, ride, and give these bills[1]
Unto the legions on the other side: [*Loud alarum.*]
Let them set on at once; for I perceive
But cold demeanour in Octavius' wing,
And sudden push gives them the overthrow.
Ride, ride, Messala: let them all come down. [*Exeunt.*]

Scene III—Another part of the field

Alarums. Enter CASSIUS *and* TITINIUS.

CAS. O, look, Titinius, look, the villains fly!
Myself have to mine own turn'd enemy:

1. *bills*] orders.

This ensign[1] here of mine was turning back;
I slew the coward, and did take it from him.

TIT. O Cassius, Brutus gave the word too early;
Who, having some advantage on Octavius,
Took it too eagerly: his soldiers fell to spoil,
Whilst we by Antony are all enclosed.

Enter PINDARUS.

PIN. Fly further off, my lord, fly further off;
Mark Antony is in your tents, my lord:
Fly, therefore, noble Cassius, fly far off.

CAS. This hill is far enough. Look, look, Titinius;
Are those my tents where I perceive the fire?

TIT. They are, my lord.

CAS. Titinius, if thou lovest me,
Mount thou my horse and hide thy spurs in him,
Till he have brought thee up to yonder troops
And here again; that I may rest assured
Whether yond troops are friend or enemy.

TIT. I will be here again, even with a thought.[2] [*Exit.*]

CAS. Go, Pindarus, get higher on that hill;
My sight was ever thick;[3] regard Titinius,
And tell me what thou notest about the field.
[*Pindarus ascends the hill.*]
This day I breathed first: time is come round,
And where I did begin, there shall I end;
My life is run his compass. Sirrah, what news?

PIN. [*Above.*] O my lord!

CAS. What news?

PIN. [*Above.*] Titinius is enclosed round about
With horsemen, that make to him on the spur;
Yet he spurs on. Now they are almost on him.
Now, Titinius! Now some light.[4] O, he lights too.
He's ta'en. [*Shout.*] And, hark! they shout for joy.

CAS. Come down; behold no more.
O, coward that I am, to live so long,
To see my best friend ta'en before my face!

1. *ensign*] standard-bearer.
2. *even with a thought*] quick as thought.
3. *thick*] dim.
4. *light*] dismount.

PINDARUS *descends.*

Come hither, sirrah:
In Parthia did I take thee prisoner;
And then I swore thee, saving of thy life,
That whatsoever I did bid thee do,
Thou shouldst attempt it. Come now, keep thine oath;
Now be a freeman; and with this good sword,
That ran through Caesar's bowels, search this bosom.
Stand not to answer: here, take thou the hilts;[5]
And when my face is covered, as 't is now,
Guide thou the sword. [*Pindarus stabs him.*] Caesar, thou art revenged,
Even with this sword that kill'd thee. [*Dies.*]

PIN. So, I am free; yet would not so have been,
Durst I have done my will. O Cassius!
Far from this country Pindarus shall run,
Where never Roman shall take note of him. [*Exit.*]

Re-enter TITINIUS *with* MESSALA.

MES. It is but change,[6] Titinius; for Octavius
Is overthrown by noble Brutus' power,
As Cassius' legions are by Antony.
TIT. These tidings will well comfort Cassius.
MES. Where did you leave him?
TIT. All disconsolate,
With Pindarus his bondman, on this hill.
MES. Is not that he that lies upon the ground?
TIT. He lies not like the living. O my heart!
MES. Is not that he?
TIT. No, this was he, Messala,
But Cassius is no more. O setting sun,
As in thy red rays thou dost sink to night,
So in his red blood Cassius' day is set,
The sun of Rome is set! Our day is gone;
Clouds, dews and dangers come; our deeds are done!
Mistrust of my success hath done this deed.
MES. Mistrust of good success[7] hath done this deed.
O hateful error, melancholy's child,

5. *hilts*] handle.
6. *change*] i.e., of fortune.
7. *Mistrust of good success*] doubt of a favorable result.

Why dost thou show to the apt[8] thoughts of men
The things that are not? O error, soon conceived,
Thou never comest unto a happy birth,
But kill'st the mother that engender'd thee!

TIT. What, Pindarus! where art thou, Pindarus?

MES. Seek him, Titinius, whilst I go to meet
The noble Brutus, thrusting this report
Into his ears: I may say "thrusting" it,
For piercing steel and darts envenomed
Shall be as welcome to the ears of Brutus
As tidings of this sight.

TIT. Hie you, Messala,
And I will seek for Pindarus the while. [*Exit* MESSALA.]
Why didst thou send me forth, brave Cassius?
Did I not meet thy friends? and did not they
Put on my brows this wreath of victory,
And bid me give it thee? Didst thou not hear their shouts?
Alas, thou hast misconstrued every thing!
But, hold thee, take this garland on thy brow;
Thy Brutus bid me give it thee, and I
Will do his bidding. Brutus, come apace,
And see how I regarded Caius Cassius.
By your leave, gods: this is a Roman's part:
Come, Cassius' sword, and find Titinius' heart. [*Kills himself.*]

Alarum. Re-enter MESSALA, *with* BRUTUS, *young* CATO, *and others.*

BRU. Where, where, Messala, doth his body lie?

MES. Lo, yonder, and Titinius mourning it.

BRU. Titinius' face is upward.

CATO. He is slain.

BRU. O Julius Caesar, thou art mighty yet!
Thy spirit walks abroad, and turns our swords
In our own proper entrails. [*Low alarums.*]

CATO. Brave Titinius!
Look, whether he have not crown'd dead Cassius!

BRU. Are yet two Romans living such as these?
The last of all the Romans, fare thee well!
It is impossible that ever Rome
Should breed thy fellow. Friends, I owe moe tears
To this dead man than you shall see me pay.

8. *apt*] impressionable.

I shall find time, Cassius, I shall find time.
Come therefore, and to Thasos[9] send his body:
His funerals shall not be in our camp,
Lest it discomfort[10] us. Lucilius, come,
And come, young Cato: let us to the field.
Labeo and Flavius, set our battles on.[11]
'T is three o'clock; and, Romans, yet ere night
We shall try fortune in a second fight. [*Exeunt.*]

Scene IV—Another part of the field

Alarum. Enter, fighting, Soldiers *of both armies; then* BRUTUS, *young* CATO, LUCILIUS, *and others.*

BRU. Yet, countrymen, O, yet hold up your heads!
CATO. What bastard doth not? Who will go with me?
I will proclaim my name about the field.
I am the son of Marcus Cato, ho!
A foe to tyrants, and my country's friend;
I am the son of Marcus Cato, ho!
BRU. And I am Brutus, Marcus Brutus, I;
Brutus, my country's friend; know me for Brutus! [*Exit.*]
LUCIL. O young and noble Cato, art thou down?
Why, now thou diest as bravely as Titinius,
And mayst be honour'd, being Cato's son.
FIRST SOLD. Yield, or thou diest.
LUCIL. Only I yield to die:
[*Offering money.*] There is so much that thou wilt kill me straight;
Kill Brutus, and be honour'd in his death.
FIRST SOLD. We must not. A noble prisoner!
SEC. SOLD. Room, ho! Tell Antony, Brutus is ta'en.
FIRST SOLD. I'll tell the news. Here comes the general.

Enter ANTONY.

Brutus is ta'en, Brutus is ta'en, my lord.

9. *Thasos*] an island in the Aegean Sea, not far from the battlefield of Philippi.
10. *discomfort*] discourage.
11. *set our battles on*] advance our army.

ANT. Where is he?

LUCIL. Safe, Antony; Brutus is safe enough:
I dare assure thee that no enemy
Shall ever take alive the noble Brutus:
The gods defend him from so great a shame!
When you do find him, or alive or dead,
He will be found like Brutus, like himself.

ANT. This is not Brutus, friend, but, I assure you,
A prize no less in worth: keep this man safe,
Give him all kindness: I had rather have
Such men my friends than enemies. Go on,
And see whether Brutus be alive or dead,
And bring us word unto Octavius' tent
How every thing is chanced. [*Exeunt.*]

Scene V—Another part of the field

Enter BRUTUS, DARDANIUS, CLITUS, STRATO, *and* VOLUMNIUS.

BRU. Come, poor remains of friends, rest on this rock.

CLI. Statilius show'd the torch-light,[1] but, my lord,
He came not back: he is or ta'en or slain.

BRU. Sit thee down, Clitus: slaying is the word;
It is a deed in fashion. Hark thee, Clitus. [*Whispering.*]

CLI. What, I, my lord? No, not for all the world.

BRU. Peace then, no words.

CLI. I'll rather kill myself.

BRU. Hark thee, Dardanius. [*Whispering.*]

DAR. Shall I do such a deed?

CLI. O Dardanius!

DAR. O Clitus!

CLI. What ill request did Brutus make to thee?

DAR. To kill him, Clitus. Look, he meditates.

CLI. Now is that noble vessel full of grief,
That it runs over even at his eyes.

BRU. Come hither, good Volumnius; list a word.

VOL. What says my lord?

BRU. Why, this, Volumnius:

1. *show'd the torch-light*] signaled.

The ghost of Caesar hath appear'd to me
Two several times by night; at Sardis once,
And this last night here in Philippi fields:
I know my hour is come.

VOL. Not so, my lord.

BRU. Nay, I am sure it is, Volumnius.
Thou seest the world, Volumnius, how it goes;
Our enemies have beat us to the pit:[2] [*Low alarums.*]
It is more worthy to leap in ourselves
Than tarry till they push us. Good Volumnius,
Thou know'st that we two went to school together:
Even for that our love of old, I prithee,
Hold thou my sword-hilts, whilst I run on it.

VOL. That's not an office for a friend, my lord. [*Alarum still.*]

CLI. Fly, fly, my lord; there is no tarrying here.

BRU. Farewell to you; and you; and you, Volumnius.
Strato, thou hast been all this while asleep;
Farewell to thee too, Strato. Countrymen,
My heart doth joy that yet in all my life
I found no man but he was true to me.
I shall have glory by this losing day,
More than Octavius and Mark Antony
By this vile conquest shall attain unto.
So, fare you well at once; for Brutus' tongue
Hath almost ended his life's history:
Night hangs upon mine eyes; my bones would rest,
That have but labour'd to attain this hour.
[*Alarum. Cry within*, "Fly, fly, fly!"]

CLI. Fly, my lord, fly.

BRU. Hence! I will follow.
[*Exeunt* CLITUS, DARDANIUS, *and* VOLUMNIUS.]
I prithee, Strato, stay thou by thy lord:
Thou art a fellow of a good respect;[3]
Thy life hath had some smatch[4] of honour in it:
Hold then my sword, and turn away thy face,
While I do run upon it. Wilt thou, Strato?

STRA. Give me your hand first: fare you well, my lord.

2. *pit*] animal trap, grave.
3. *respect*] reputation.
4. *smatch*] smack, tinge.

BRU. Farewell, good Strato. [*Runs on his sword.*] Caesar, now be still:
I kill'd not thee with half so good a will. [*Dies.*]

Alarum. Retreat. Enter OCTAVIUS, ANTONY, MESSALA, LUCILIUS, *and the* Army.

OCT. What man is that?
MES. My master's man. Strato, where is thy master?
STRA. Free from the bondage you are in, Messala:
The conquerors can but make a fire of him;
For Brutus only overcame himself,
And no man else hath honour by his death.
LUCIL. So Brutus should be found. I thank thee, Brutus,
That thou hast proved Lucilius' saying true.
OCT. All that served Brutus, I will entertain them.[5]
Fellow, wilt thou bestow thy time with me?
STRA. Ay, if Messala will prefer[6] me to you.
OCT. Do so, good Messala.
MES. How died my master, Strato?
STRA. I held the sword, and he did run on it.
MES. Octavius, then take him to follow thee,
That did the latest service to my master.
ANT. This was the noblest Roman of them all:
All the conspirators, save only he,
Did that they did in envy of great Caesar;
He only, in a general honest thought[7]
And common good to all, made one of them.
His life was gentle, and the elements
So mix'd in him that Nature might stand up
And say to all the world "This was a man!"
OCT. According to his virtue let us use him,
With all respect and rites of burial.
Within my tent his bones to-night shall lie,
Most like a soldier, order'd honourably.
So call the field to rest, and let's away,
To part[8] the glories of this happy day. [*Exeunt.*]

5. *entertain them*] take them into my service.
6. *prefer*] recommend.
7. *general honest thought*] an honest concern for the public good.
8. *part*] distribute.

FICTION

THE QUEEN OF SPADES AND OTHER STORIES, Alexander Pushkin. 128pp. 28054-3
THE STORY OF AN AFRICAN FARM, Olive Schreiner. 256pp. 40165-0
FRANKENSTEIN, Mary Shelley. 176pp. 28211-2
THE JUNGLE, Upton Sinclair. 320pp. (Available in U.S. only.) 41923-1
THREE LIVES, Gertrude Stein. 176pp. (Available in U.S. only.) 28059-4
THE BODY SNATCHER AND OTHER TALES, Robert Louis Stevenson. 80pp. 41924-X
THE STRANGE CASE OF DR. JEKYLL AND MR. HYDE, Robert Louis Stevenson. 64pp. 26688-5
TREASURE ISLAND, Robert Louis Stevenson. 160pp. 27559-0
GULLIVER'S TRAVELS, Jonathan Swift. 240pp. 29273-8
THE KREUTZER SONATA AND OTHER SHORT STORIES, Leo Tolstoy. 144pp. 27805-0
THE WARDEN, Anthony Trollope. 176pp. 40076-X
FIRST LOVE AND DIARY OF A SUPERFLUOUS MAN, Ivan Turgenev. 96pp. 28775-0
FATHERS AND SONS, Ivan Turgenev. 176pp. 40073-5
ADVENTURES OF HUCKLEBERRY FINN, Mark Twain. 224pp. 28061-6
THE ADVENTURES OF TOM SAWYER, Mark Twain. 192pp. 40077-8
THE MYSTERIOUS STRANGER AND OTHER STORIES, Mark Twain. 128pp. 27069-6
HUMOROUS STORIES AND SKETCHES, Mark Twain. 80pp. 29279-7
AROUND THE WORLD IN EIGHTY DAYS, Jules Verne. 160pp. 41111-7
CANDIDE, Voltaire (François-Marie Arouet). 112pp. 26689-3
GREAT SHORT STORIES BY AMERICAN WOMEN, Candace Ward (ed.). 192pp. 28776-9
"THE COUNTRY OF THE BLIND" AND OTHER SCIENCE-FICTION STORIES, H. G. Wells. 160pp. (Not available in Europe or United Kingdom.) 29569-9
THE ISLAND OF DR. MOREAU, H. G. Wells. 112pp. (Not available in Europe or United Kingdom.) 29027-1
THE INVISIBLE MAN, H. G. Wells. 112pp. (Not available in Europe or United Kingdom.) 27071-8
THE TIME MACHINE, H. G. Wells. 80pp. (Not available in Europe or United Kingdom.) 28472-7
THE WAR OF THE WORLDS, H. G. Wells. 160pp. (Not available in Europe or United Kingdom.) 29506-0
ETHAN FROME, Edith Wharton. 96pp. 26690-7
SHORT STORIES, Edith Wharton. 128pp. 28235-X
THE AGE OF INNOCENCE, Edith Wharton. 288pp. 29803-5
THE PICTURE OF DORIAN GRAY, Oscar Wilde. 192pp. 27807-7
JACOB'S ROOM, Virginia Woolf. 144pp. (Not available in Europe or United Kingdom.) 40109-X
MONDAY OR TUESDAY: Eight Stories, Virginia Woolf. 64pp. (Not available in Europe or United Kingdom.) 29453-6

NONFICTION

POETICS, Aristotle. 64pp. 29577-X
POLITICS, Aristotle. 368pp. 41424-8
NICOMACHEAN ETHICS, Aristotle. 256pp. 40096-4
MEDITATIONS, Marcus Aurelius. 128pp. 29823-X
THE LAND OF LITTLE RAIN, Mary Austin. 96pp. 29037-9
THE DEVIL'S DICTIONARY, Ambrose Bierce. 144pp. 27542-6
THE ANALECTS, Confucius. 128pp. 28484-0
CONFESSIONS OF AN ENGLISH OPIUM EATER, Thomas De Quincey. 80pp. 28742-4
THE SOULS OF BLACK FOLK, W. E. B. Du Bois. 176pp. 28041-1

DOVER · THRIFT · EDITIONS

PLAYS

THE MIKADO, William Schwenck Gilbert. 64pp. 27268-0
FAUST, PART ONE, Johann Wolfgang von Goethe. 192pp. 28046-2
THE INSPECTOR GENERAL, Nikolai Gogol. 80pp. 28500-6
SHE STOOPS TO CONQUER, Oliver Goldsmith. 80pp. 26867-5
A DOLL'S HOUSE, Henrik Ibsen. 80pp. 27062-9
GHOSTS, Henrik Ibsen. 64pp. 29852-3
HEDDA GABLER, Henrik Ibsen. 80pp. 26469-6
THE WILD DUCK, Henrik Ibsen. 96pp. 41116-8
VOLPONE, Ben Jonson. 112pp. 28049-7
DR. FAUSTUS, Christopher Marlowe. 64pp. 28208-2
THE MISANTHROPE, Molière. 64pp. 27065-3
ANNA CHRISTIE, Eugene O'Neill. 80pp. 29985-6
BEYOND THE HORIZON, Eugene O'Neill. 96pp. 29085-9
THE EMPEROR JONES, Eugene O'Neill. 64pp. 29268-1
THE LONG VOYAGE HOME AND OTHER PLAYS, Eugene O'Neill. 80pp. 28755-6
RIGHT YOU ARE, IF YOU THINK YOU ARE, Luigi Pirandello. 64pp. (Not available in Europe or United Kingdom.) 29576-1
SIX CHARACTERS IN SEARCH OF AN AUTHOR, Luigi Pirandello. 64pp. (Not available in Europe or United Kingdom.) 29992-9
PHÈDRE, Jean Racine. 64pp. 41927-4
HANDS AROUND, Arthur Schnitzler. 64pp. 28724-6
ANTONY AND CLEOPATRA, William Shakespeare. 128pp. 40062-X
AS YOU LIKE IT, William Shakespeare. 80pp. 40432-3
HAMLET, William Shakespeare. 128pp. 27278-8
HENRY IV, William Shakespeare. 96pp. 29584-2
JULIUS CAESAR, William Shakespeare. 80pp. 26876-4
KING LEAR, William Shakespeare. 112pp. 28058-6
LOVE'S LABOUR'S LOST, William Shakespeare. 64pp. 41929-0
MACBETH, William Shakespeare. 96pp. 27802-6
MEASURE FOR MEASURE, William Shakespeare. 96pp. 40889-2
THE MERCHANT OF VENICE, William Shakespeare. 96pp. 28492-1
A MIDSUMMER NIGHT'S DREAM, William Shakespeare. 80pp. 27067-X
MUCH ADO ABOUT NOTHING, William Shakespeare. 80pp. 28272-4
OTHELLO, William Shakespeare. 112pp. 29097-2
RICHARD III, William Shakespeare. 112pp. 28747-5
ROMEO AND JULIET, William Shakespeare. 96pp. 27557-4
THE TAMING OF THE SHREW, William Shakespeare. 96pp. 29765-9
THE TEMPEST, William Shakespeare. 96pp. 40658-X
TWELFTH NIGHT; OR, WHAT YOU WILL, William Shakespeare. 80pp. 29290-8
ARMS AND THE MAN, George Bernard Shaw. 80pp. (Not available in Europe or United Kingdom.) 26476-9
HEARTBREAK HOUSE, George Bernard Shaw. 128pp. (Not available in Europe or United Kingdom.) 29291-6
PYGMALION, George Bernard Shaw. 96pp. (Available in U.S. only.) 28222-8
THE RIVALS, Richard Brinsley Sheridan. 96pp. 40433-1
THE SCHOOL FOR SCANDAL, Richard Brinsley Sheridan. 96pp. 26687-7
ANTIGONE, Sophocles. 64pp. 27804-2
OEDIPUS AT COLONUS, Sophocles. 64pp. 40659-8
OEDIPUS REX, Sophocles. 64pp. 26877-2